PRAISE FOR *IF I STAY*

AN IMPOSSIBLE CHOICE

How am I supposed to decide this? How can I possibly stay without Mom and Dad? How can I leave without Teddy? Or Adam? This is too much. I don't even understand how it all works, why I'm here in the state that I'm in or how to get out of it if I wanted to. If I were to say, *I want to wake up*, would I wake up right now? I already tried snapping my heels to find Teddy and trying to beam myself to Hawaii, and that didn't work. This seems a whole lot more complicated.

But in spite of that, I believe it's true. I hear the nurse's words again. I am running the show. Everyone is waiting on me.

I decide. I know this now.

And this terrifies me more than anything else that has happened today.

ALSO BY GAYLE FORMAN

IF I
STAY

IF I
STAY

GAYLE FORMAN

PENGUIN BOOKS

Penguin Books
An imprint of Penguin Random House LLC, New York

First published in the United States of America by Dutton Books,
an imprint of Penguin Random House LLC, 2009
Published by Speak, an imprint of Penguin Random House LLC, 2010
This edition published by Penguin Books, an imprint of Penguin Random House LLC, 2019

Visit us online at penguinrandomhouse.com

THE LIBRARY OF CONGRESS HAS CATALOGED THE DUTTON BOOKS EDITION AS FOLLOWS:
Forman, Gayle.
If I stay: a novel / by Gayle Forman.
p. cm.
Summary: While in a coma following an automobile accident that killed her parents
and younger brother, seventeen-year-old Mia, a gifted cellist, weighs
whether to live with her grief or join her family in death.
ISBN: 978-0-585-42103-0 (hc)
[1. Coma—Fiction. 2. Death—Fiction. 3. Medical care—Fiction. 4. Violoncellists—Fiction.
5. Family life—Oregon—Fiction. 6. Oregon—Fiction.] I. Title.
PZ7.F75876If 2009
[Fic]—dc22 2008023938

This edition ISBN 9781984836502

Printed in the United States of America

1 3 5 7 9 10 8 6 4 2

FOR NICK

Finally . . . Always

IF I

STAY

Everyone thinks it was because of the snow. And in a way, I suppose that's true.

I wake up this morning to a thin blanket of white covering our front lawn. It isn't even an inch, but in this part of Oregon a slight dusting brings everything to a standstill as the one snowplow in the county gets busy clearing the roads. It is wet water that drops from the sky—and drops and drops and drops—not the frozen kind.

It is enough snow to cancel school. My little brother, Teddy, lets out a war whoop when Mom's

AM radio announces the closures. "Snow day!" he bellows. "Dad, let's go make a snowman."

My dad smiles and taps on his pipe. He started smoking one recently as part of this whole 1950s, *Father Knows Best* retro kick he is on. He also wears bow ties. I am never quite clear on whether all this is sartorial or sardonic—Dad's way of announcing that he used to be a punker but is now a middle-school English teacher, or if becoming a teacher has actually turned my dad into this genuine throwback. But I like the smell of the pipe tobacco. It is sweet and smoky, and reminds me of winters and woodstoves.

"You can make a valiant try," Dad tells Teddy. "But it's hardly sticking to the roads. Maybe you should consider a snow amoeba."

I can tell Dad is happy. Barely an inch of snow means that all the schools in the county are closed, including my high school and the middle school where Dad works, so it's an unexpected day off for him, too. My mother, who works for a travel agent in town, clicks off the radio and pours herself a second cup of coffee. "Well, if you lot are playing hooky today, no way I'm going to work. It's simply not right." She picks up the telephone to call in. When she's done, she looks at us. "Should I make breakfast?"

Dad and I guffaw at the same time. Mom makes cereal and toast. Dad's the cook in the family.

Pretending not to hear us, she reaches into the cabinet for a box of Bisquick. "Please. How hard can it be? Who wants pancakes?"

"I do! I do!" Teddy yells. "Can we have chocolate chips in them?"

"I don't see why not," Mom replies.

"Woo hoo!" Teddy yelps, waving his arms in the air.

"You have far too much energy for this early in the morning," I tease. I turn to Mom. "Maybe you shouldn't let Teddy drink so much coffee."

"I've switched him to decaf," Mom volleys back. "He's just naturally exuberant."

"As long as you're not switching *me* to decaf," I say.

"That would be child abuse," Dad says.

Mom hands me a steaming mug and the newspaper.

"There's a nice picture of your young man in there," she says.

"Really? A picture?"

"Yep. It's about the most we've seen of him since summer," Mom says, giving me a sidelong glance with her eyebrow arched, her version of a soul-searching stare.

"I know," I say, and then without meaning to, I sigh. Adam's band, Shooting Star, is on an upward spiral, which is a great thing—mostly.

"Ah, fame, wasted on the youth," Dad says, but he's smiling. I know he's excited for Adam. Proud even.

I leaf through the newspaper to the calendar section. There's a small blurb about Shooting Star, with an even smaller picture of the four of them, next to a big article about Bikini and a huge picture of the band's lead singer: punk-rock diva Brooke Vega. The bit about them basically says that local band Shooting Star is opening for Bikini on the Portland leg of Bikini's national tour. It doesn't mention the even-bigger-to-me news that last night Shooting Star headlined at a club in Seattle and, according to the text Adam sent me at midnight, sold out the place.

"Are you going tonight?" Dad asks.

"I was planning to. It depends if they shut down the whole state on account of the snow."

"It *is* approaching a blizzard," Dad says, pointing to a single snowflake floating its way to the earth.

"I'm also supposed to rehearse with some pianist from the college that Professor Christie dug up." Professor Christie, a retired music teacher at the university who I've been working with for the last few years, is always looking for victims for me to play with. "Keep you sharp so you can show all those Juilliard snobs how it's really done," she says.

I haven't gotten into Juilliard yet, but my audition went really well. The Bach suite and the Shostakovich had both flown out of me like never before, like my fingers were just an extension of the strings and bow. When I'd finished playing, panting, my legs shaking from pressing together so hard, one judge had clapped a little, which I guess doesn't happen very often. As I'd shuffled out, that same judge had told me that it had been a long time since the school had "seen an Oregon country girl." Professor Christie had taken that to mean a guaranteed acceptance. I wasn't so sure that was true. And I wasn't 100 percent sure that I wanted it to be true. Just like with Shooting Star's meteoric rise, my admission to Juilliard—if it happens—will create certain complications, or, more accurately, would compound the complications that have already cropped up in the last few months.

"I need more coffee. Anyone else?" Mom asks, hovering over me with the ancient percolator.

I sniff the coffee, the rich, black, oily French roast we all prefer. The smell alone perks me up.

"I'm pondering going back to bed," I say. "My cello's at school, so I can't even practice."

"Not practice? For twenty-four hours? Be still, my broken heart," Mom says. Though she has acquired a taste for classical music over the years—"it's like learning to appreciate a stinky cheese"—she's been a not-always-delighted captive audience for many of my marathon rehearsals.

I hear a crash and a boom coming from upstairs. Teddy is pounding on his drum kit. It used to belong to Dad. Back when he'd played drums in a big-in-our-town, unknown-anywhere-else band, back when he'd worked at a record store.

Dad grins at Teddy's noise, and seeing that, I feel a familiar pang. I know it's silly but I have always wondered if Dad is disappointed that I didn't become a rock chick. I'd meant to. Then, in third grade, I'd wandered over to the cello in music class—it looked almost human to me. It looked like if you played it, it would tell you secrets, so I started playing. It's been almost ten years now and I haven't stopped.

"So much for going back to sleep," Mom yells over Teddy's noise.

"What do you know, the snow's already melting."

Dad says, puffing on his pipe. I go to the back door and peek outside. A patch of sunlight has broken through the clouds, and I can hear the hiss of the ice melting. I close the door and go back to the table.

"I think the county overreacted," I say.

"Maybe. But they can't un-cancel school. Horse is already out of the barn, and I already called in for the day off," Mom says.

"Indeed. But we might take advantage of this unexpected boon and go somewhere," Dad says. "Take a drive. Visit Henry and Willow." Henry and Willow are some of Mom and Dad's old music friends who'd also had a kid and decided to start behaving like grown-ups. They live in a big old farmhouse. Henry does Web stuff from the barn they converted into a home office and Willow works at a nearby hospital. They have a baby girl. That's the real reason Mom and Dad want to go out there. Teddy having just turned eight and me being seventeen means that we are long past giving off that sour-milk smell that makes adults melt.

"We can stop at BookBarn on the way back," Mom says, as if to entice me. BookBarn is a giant, dusty old used-book store. In the back they keep a stash of twenty-five-cent classical records that nobody ever seems to buy except me. I keep a pile of them hidden under my bed. A collection of classical records is not the kind of thing you advertise.

I've shown them to Adam, but that was only after we'd already been together for five months. I'd expected him to laugh. He's such the cool guy with his pegged jeans and black low-tops, his effortlessly beat-up punk-rock tees and his subtle tattoos. He is so not the kind of guy to end up with someone like me. Which was why when I'd first spotted him watching me at the music studios at school two years ago, I'd been convinced he was making fun of me and I'd hidden from him. Anyhow, he hadn't laughed. It turned out he had a dusty collection of punk-rock records under his bed.

"We can also stop by Gran and Gramps for an early dinner," Dad says, already reaching for the phone. "We'll have you back in plenty of time to get to Portland," he adds as he dials.

"I'm in," I say. It isn't the lure of BookBarn, or the fact that Adam is on tour, or that my best friend, Kim, is busy doing yearbook stuff. It isn't even that my cello is at school or that I could stay home and watch TV or sleep. I'd actually rather go off with my family. This is another thing you don't advertise about yourself, but Adam gets that, too.

"Teddy," Dad calls. "Get dressed. We're going on an adventure."

Teddy finishes off his drum solo with a crash of cymbals. A moment later he's bounding into the kitchen fully dressed, as if he'd pulled on his clothes while careening down the steep wooden staircase of our drafty Victorian house. "School's out for summer . . ." he sings.

"Alice Cooper?" Dad asks. "Have we no standards? At least sing the Ramones."

"School's out forever," Teddy sings over Dad's protests.

"Ever the optimist," I say.

Mom laughs. She puts a plate of slightly charred pancakes down on the kitchen table. "Eat up, family."

8:17 A.M.

We pile into the car, a rusting Buick that was already old when Gran gave it to us after Teddy was born. Mom and Dad offer to let me drive, but I say no. Dad slips behind the wheel. He likes to drive now. He'd stubbornly refused to get a license for years, insisting on riding his bike everywhere. Back when he played music, his ban on driving meant that his bandmates were the ones stuck behind the wheel on tours. They used to roll their eyes at him. Mom had done more than that. She'd pestered, cajoled, and sometimes yelled at Dad to get a license, but he'd insisted that he preferred pedal power. "Well, then you better get to work on building a bike that can hold a family of three and keep us dry when it rains," she'd demanded. To which Dad always had laughed and said that he'd get on that.

But when Mom had gotten pregnant with Teddy, she'd put her foot down. Enough, she said. Dad seemed to understand that something had changed. He'd stopped arguing and had gotten a driver's license. He'd also gone back to school to get his teaching certificate. I guess it was okay to be in arrested development with one kid. But with two, time to grow up. Time to start wearing a bow tie.

He has one on this morning, along with a flecked sport coat and vintage wingtips. "Dressed for the snow, I see," I say.

"I'm like the post office," Dad replies, scraping the snow off the car with one of Teddy's plastic dinosaurs that are scattered on the lawn. "Neither sleet nor rain nor a half inch of snow will compel me to dress like a lumberjack."

"Hey, my relatives were lumberjacks," Mom warns. "No making fun of the white-trash woodsmen."

"Wouldn't dream of it," Dad replies. "Just making stylistic contrasts."

Dad has to turn the ignition over a few times before the car chokes to life. As usual, there is a battle for stereo dominance. Mom wants NPR. Dad wants Frank Sinatra. Teddy wants SpongeBob SquarePants. I want the classical-music station, but recognizing that I'm the only classical fan in the family, I am willing to compromise with Shooting Star.

Dad brokers the deal. "Seeing as we're missing school today, we ought to listen to the news for a while so we don't become ignoramuses—"

"I believe that's ignoramusi," Mom says.

Dad rolls his eyes and clasps his hand over Mom's and clears his throat in that schoolteachery way of his. "As I was saying, NPR first, and then when the news is over, the classical station. Teddy, we will not torture you with that. You can use the Discman," Dad says, starting to disconnect the portable player he's rigged to the car radio. "But you are not allowed to play Alice Cooper in my car. I forbid it." Dad reaches into the glove box to examine what's inside. "How about Jonathan Richman?"

"I want SpongeBob. It's in the machine," Teddy

shouts, bouncing up and down and pointing to the Discman. The chocolate-chip pancakes dowsed in syrup have clearly only enhanced his hyper excitement.

"Son, you break my heart," Dad jokes. Both Teddy and I were raised on the goofy tunes of Jonathan Richman, who is Mom and Dad's musical patron saint.

Once the musical selections have been made, we are off. The road has some patches of snow, but mostly it's just wet. But this is Oregon. The roads are always wet. Mom used to joke that it was when the road was dry that people ran into trouble. "They get cocky, throw caution to the wind, drive like assholes. The cops have a field day doling out speeding tickets."

I lean my head against the car window, watching the scenery zip by, a tableau of dark green fir trees dotted with snow, wispy strands of white fog, and heavy gray storm clouds up above. It's so warm in the car that the windows keep fogging up, and I draw little squiggles in the condensation.

When the news is over, we turn to the classical station. I hear the first few bars of Beethoven's Cello Sonata no. 3, which was the very piece I was supposed to be working on this afternoon. It feels like some kind of cosmic coincidence. I concentrate on the notes, imagining myself playing, feeling grateful for this chance to practice, happy to be in a warm car with my sonata and my family. I close my eyes.

You wouldn't expect the radio to work afterward. But it does.

The car is eviscerated. The impact of a four-ton pickup truck going sixty miles an hour plowing straight into the passenger side had the force of an atom bomb. It tore off the doors, sent the front-side passenger seat through the driver's-side window. It flipped the chassis, bouncing it across the road and ripped the engine apart as if it were no stronger than a spiderweb. It tossed wheels and hubcaps deep into the forest. It ignited bits of the gas tank, so that now tiny flames lap at the wet road.

And there was so much noise. A symphony of grinding, a chorus of popping, an aria of exploding, and finally, the sad clapping of hard metal cutting into soft trees. Then it went quiet, except for this: Beethoven's Cello Sonata no. 3, still playing. The car radio somehow still is attached to a battery and so Beethoven is broadcasting into the once-again tranquil February morning.

At first I figure everything is fine. For one, I can still hear the Beethoven. Then there's the fact that I am standing here in a ditch on the side of the road. When I look down, the jean skirt, cardigan sweater, and the black boots I put on this morning all look the same as they did when we left the house.

I climb up the embankment to get a better look at the car. It isn't even a car anymore. It's a metal skeleton, without seats, without passengers. Which means the rest of my family must have been thrown from the car like me. I brush off my hands onto my skirt and walk into the road to find them.

I see Dad first. Even from several feet away, I can make out the protrusion of the pipe in his jacket pocket. "Dad," I call, but as I walk toward him, the pavement grows slick and there are gray chunks of what looks like cauliflower. I know what I'm see-ing right away but it somehow does not immedi-ately connect back to my father. What springs into my mind are those news reports about tornadoes or fires, how they'll ravage one house but leave the one next door intact. Pieces of my father's brain are on the asphalt. But his pipe is in his left breast pocket.

I find Mom next. There's almost no blood on her, but her lips are already blue and the whites of her eyes are completely red, like a ghoul from a low-budget monster movie. She seems totally unreal. And it is the sight of her looking like some preposterous zombie that sends a hummingbird of panic ricocheting through me.

I need to find Teddy! Where is he? I spin around, suddenly frantic, like the time I lost him for ten minutes at the grocery store. I'd been convinced he'd been kidnapped. Of course, it had turned out that he'd wandered over to inspect the candy aisle. When I found him, I hadn't been sure whether to hug him or yell at him.

I run back toward the ditch where I came from and I see a hand sticking out. "Teddy! I'm right here!" I call. "Reach up. I'll pull you out." But when I get closer, I see the metal glint of a silver bracelet with tiny cello and guitar charms. Adam gave it to me for my seventeenth birthday. It's *my* bracelet. I was wearing it this morning. I look down at my wrist. I'm *still* wearing it now.

I edge closer and now I know that it's not Teddy lying there. It's me. The blood from my chest has seeped through my shirt, skirt, and sweater, and is now pooling like paint drops on the virgin snow. One of my legs is askew, the skin and muscle peeled away so that I can see white streaks of bone. My eyes are closed, and my dark brown hair is wet and rusty with blood.

I spin away. This isn't right. This cannot be happening. We are a family, going on a drive. This isn't real. I must have fallen asleep in the car. *No! Stop. Please stop. Please wake up!* I scream into the chilly air. It's cold. My breath should smoke. It doesn't. I stare down at my wrist, the one that looks fine, untouched by blood and gore, and I pinch as hard as I can.

I don't feel a thing.

I have had nightmares before—falling nightmares, playing-a-cello-recital-without-knowing-the-music nightmares, breakup-with-Adam nightmares—but I have always been able to command myself to open my eyes, to lift my head from the pillow, to halt the horror movie playing behind my closed lids. I try again. *Wake up!* I scream. *Wake up! Wakeupwakeup-wakeup!* But I can't. I don't.

Then I hear something. It's the music. I can still hear the music. So I concentrate on that. I finger the notes of Beethoven's Cello Sonata no. 3 with my hands, as I often do when I listen to pieces I am working on. Adam calls it "air cello." He's always asking me if one day we can play a duet, him on air guitar, me on air cello. "When we're done, we can thrash our air instruments," he jokes. "You know you want to."

I play, just focusing on that, until the last bit of life in the car dies, and the music goes with it.

It isn't long after that the sirens come.

9:23 A.M.

Am I dead?

I actually have to ask myself this.

Am I dead?

At first it seemed obvious that I am. That the standing-here-watching part was temporary, an intermission before the bright light and the life-flashing-before-me business that would transport me to wherever I'm going next.

Except the paramedics are here now, along with the police and the fire department. Someone has put a sheet over my father. And a fireman is zipping Mom up into a plastic bag. I hear him discuss her with another firefighter, who looks like he can't be more than eighteen. The older one explains to the rookie that Mom was probably hit first and killed instantly, explaining the lack of blood. "Immediate cardiac arrest," he says.

"When your heart can't pump blood, you don't really bleed. You seep."

I can't think about that, about Mom seeping. So instead I think how fitting it is that she was hit first, that she was the one to buffer us from the blow. It wasn't her choice, obviously, but it was her way.

But am I dead? The me who is lying on the edge of the road, my leg hanging down into the gulley, is surrounded by a team of men and women who are performing frantic ablutions over me and plugging my veins with I do not know what. I'm half naked, the paramedics having ripped open the top of my shirt. One of my breasts is exposed. Embarrassed, I look away.

The police have lit flares along the perimeter of the scene and are instructing cars in both directions to turn back, the road is closed. The police politely offer alternate routes, back roads that will take people where they need to be.

They must have places to go, the people in these cars, but a lot of them don't turn back. They climb out of their cars, hugging themselves against the cold. They appraise the scene. And then they look away, some of them crying, one woman throwing up into the ferns on the side of the road. And even though they don't know who we are or what has happened, they pray for us. I can feel them praying.

Which also makes me think I'm dead. That and the fact my body seems to be completely numb, though to look at me, at the leg that the 60 mph asphalt exfoliant has pared down to the bone, I should be in agony. And I'm not crying, either, even though I *know* that something unthinkable has just happened to my family. We are like Humpty Dumpty and all these king's horses and all these king's men cannot put us back together again.

I am pondering these things when the medic with the freckles and red hair who has been working on me answers my question. "Her Glasgow Coma is an eight. Let's bag her now!" she screams.

She and the lantern-jawed medic snake a tube down my throat, attach a bag with a bulb to it, and start pumping. "What's the ETA for Life Flight?"

"Ten minutes," answers the medic. "It takes twenty to get back to town."

"We're going to get her there in fifteen if you have to speed like a fucking demon."

I can tell what the guy is thinking. That it won't do me any good if they get into a crash, and I have to agree. But he doesn't say anything. Just clenches his jaw. They load me into the ambulance; the red-head climbs into the back with me. She pumps my bag with one hand, adjusts my IV and my monitors with the other. Then she smooths a lock of hair from my forehead.

"You hang in there," she tells me.

⁓

I played my first recital when I was ten. I'd been playing cello for two years at that point. At first, just at school, as part of the music program. It was a fluke that they even had a cello; they're very expensive and fragile. But some old literature professor from the university had died and bequeathed his Hamburg to our school. It mostly sat in the corner. Most kids wanted to learn to play guitar or saxophone.

When I announced to Mom and Dad that I was going to become a cellist, they both burst out laughing. They apologized about it later, claiming that the image of pint-size me with such a hulking instrument between my spindly legs had made them crack up. Once they'd realized I was serious, they immediately swallowed their giggles and put on supportive faces.

But their reaction still stung—in ways that I never told them about, and in ways that I'm not sure they would've understood even if I had. Dad sometimes joked that the hospital where I was born must have accidentally swapped babies because I look nothing like the rest of my family. They are all blond and fair and I'm like their negative image, brown hair and dark eyes. But as I got older, Dad's hospital joke took on more meaning than I think he intended. Sometimes I did feel like I came from a different tribe. I was not like my outgoing, ironic dad or my tough-chick mom. And as if to seal the deal, instead of learning to play electric guitar, I'd gone and chosen the cello.

But in my family, playing music was still more important than the type of music you played, so when after a few months it became clear that my love for the cello was no passing crush, my parents rented me one so I could practice at home. Rusty scales and triads led to first attempts at "Twinkle, Twinkle, Little Star" that eventually gave way to basic études until I was playing Bach suites. My middle school didn't have much of a music program, so Mom found me a private teacher, a college student who came over once a week. Over the years there was a revolving batch of students who taught me, and then, as my skills surpassed theirs, my student teachers played with me.

This continued until ninth grade, when Dad,

who'd known Professor Christie from when he'd worked at the music store, asked if she might be willing to offer me private lessons. She agreed to listen to me play, not expecting much, but as a favor to Dad, she later told me. She and Dad listened downstairs while I was up in my room practicing a Vivaldi sonata. When I came down for dinner, she offered to take over my training.

My first recital, though, was years before I met her. It was at a hall in town, a place that usually showcased local bands, so the acoustics were terrible for unamplified classical. I was playing a cello solo from Tchaikovsky's "Dance of the Sugar Plum Fairy."

Standing backstage, listening to other kids play scratchy violin and clunky piano compositions, I'd almost chickened out. I'd run to the stage door and huddled on the stoop outside, hyperventilating into my hands. My student teacher had flown into a minor panic and had sent out a search party.

Dad found me. He was just starting his hipster-to-square transformation, so he was wearing a vintage suit, with a studded leather belt and black ankle boots.

"You okay, Mia Oh-My-Uh?" he asked, sitting down next to me on the steps.

I shook my head, too ashamed to talk.

"What's up?"

"I can't do it," I cried.

Dad cocked one of his bushy eyebrows and stared at me with his gray-blue eyes. I felt like some mysterious foreign species he was observing and trying to figure out. He'd been playing in bands forever. Obviously, he *never* got something as lame as stage fright.

"Well, that would be a shame," Dad said. "I've got a dandy of a recital present for you. Better than flowers."

"Give it to someone else. I can't go out there. I'm not like you or Mom or even Teddy." Teddy was just six months old at that point, but it was already clear that he had more personality, more verve, than I ever would. And of course, he was blond and blue-eyed. Even if he weren't, he'd been born in a birthing center, not a hospital, so there was no chance of an accidental baby swapping.

"It's true," Dad mused. "When Teddy gave his first harp concert, he was cool as cucumber. Such a prodigy."

I laughed through my tears. Dad put a gentle arm around my shoulder. "You know that I used to get the most ferocious jitters before a show."

I looked at Dad, who always seemed absolutely sure of everything in the world. "You're just saying that."

He shook his head. "No, I'm not. It was god-awful. And I was the drummer, way in the back. No one even paid any attention to me."

"So what did you do?" I asked.

"He got wasted," Mom interjected, poking her head out the stage door. She was wearing a black vinyl miniskirt, a red tank top, and Teddy, droolingly happy from his Baby Björn. "A pair of forty-ouncers before the show. I don't recommend that for you."

"Your mother is probably right," Dad said. "Social services frowns on drunk ten-year-olds. Besides, when I dropped my drumsticks and puked onstage, it was punk. If you drop your bow and smell like a brewery, it will look gauche. You classical-music people are so snobby that way."

Now I was laughing. I was still scared, but it was somehow comforting to think that maybe stage fright was a trait I'd inherited from Dad; I wasn't just some foundling, after all.

"What if I mess it up? What if I'm terrible?"

"I've got news for you, Mia. There's going

to be all kinds of terrible in there, so you won't really stand out," Mom said. Teddy gave a squeal of agreement.

"But seriously, how do you get over the jitters?"

Dad was still smiling but I could tell he had turned serious because he slowed down his speech. "You don't. You just work through it. You just hang in there."

So I went on. I didn't blaze through the piece. I didn't achieve glory or get a standing ovation, but I didn't muck it up entirely, either. And after the recital, I got my present. It was sitting in the passenger seat of the car, looking as human as that cello I'd been drawn to two years earlier. It wasn't a rental. It was mine.

10:12 A.M.

When my ambulance gets to the nearest hospital—not the one in my hometown but a small local place that looks more like an old-age home than a medical center—the medics rush me inside. "I think we've got a collapsed lung. Get a chest tube in her and move her out!" the nice red-haired medic screams as she passes me off to a team of nurses and doctors.

"Where's the rest?" asks a bearded guy in scrubs.

"Other driver suffering mild concussions, being treated at the scene. Parents DOA. Boy, approximately seven years old, just behind us."

I let out a huge exhale, as though I've been holding my breath for the last twenty minutes. After seeing myself in that ditch, I had not been able to look for Teddy. If he were like Mom and Dad, like me, I . . . I didn't want to even think about it. But he isn't. He is alive.

They take me into a small room with bright lights. A doctor dabs some orange stuff onto the side of my chest and then rams a small plastic tube in me. Another doctor shines a flashlight into my eye. "Nonresponsive," he tells the nurse. "The chopper's here. Get her to Trauma. Now!"

They rush me out of the ER and into the elevator. I have to jog to keep up. Right before the doors close, I notice that Willow is here. Which is odd. We were meant to be visiting her and Henry and the baby at home. Did she get called in because of the snow? Because of us? She rushes around the hospital hall, her face a mask of concentration. I don't think she even knows it is us yet. Maybe she even tried to call, left a message on Mom's cell phone, apologizing that there'd been an emergency and she wouldn't be home for our visit.

The elevator opens right onto the roof. A helicopter, its blades swooshing the air, sits in the middle of a big red circle.

I've never been in a helicopter before. My best friend, Kim, has. She went on an aerial flight over Mount St. Helens once with her uncle, a big-shot photographer for *National Geographic.*

"There he was, talking about the post-volcanic flora and I puked right on him," Kim told me in homeroom the next day. She still looked a little green from the experience.

Kim is on yearbook and has hopes of becoming a photographer. Her uncle had taken her on this trip as a favor, to nurture her budding talent. "I even got some on his cameras," Kim lamented. "I'll never be a photographer now."

"There are all kinds of different photographers," I told her. "You don't necessarily need to go flying around in helicopters."

Kim laughed. "That's good. Because I'm never going on a helicopter again—and don't you, either!"

I want to tell Kim that sometimes you don't have a choice in the matter.

The hatch in the helicopter is opened, and my stretcher with all its tubes and lines is loaded in. I climb in behind it. A medic bounds in next to me, still pumping the little plastic bulb that is apparently breathing for me. Once we lift off, I understand why Kim got so queasy. A helicopter is not like an airplane, a smooth fast bullet. A helicopter is more like a hockey puck, bounced through the sky. Up and down, side to side. I have no idea how these people can work on me, can read the small computer printouts, can drive this thing while they communicate about me through headsets, how they can do any of it with the chopper chopping around.

The helicopter hits an air pocket and by all rights it should make me queasy. But I don't feel anything, at least the me who's a bystander here does not. And the me on the stretcher doesn't seem to feel anything, either. Again I have to wonder if I'm dead but then I tell myself no. They would not have loaded me on this helicopter, would not be flying me across the lush forests if I were dead.

Also, if I were dead, I like to think Mom and Dad would've come for me by now.

I can see the time on the control panel. It's 10:37. I wonder what's happening back down on the ground. Has Willow figured out who the emergency is? Has anyone phoned my grandparents? They live one town over from us, and I was looking forward to dinner with them. Gramps fishes and he smokes his own salmon and oysters, and we would've probably eaten that with Gran's homemade thick brown beer bread. Then Gran would've taken Teddy over to the giant recycling bins in town and let him swim around for magazines. Lately, he's had a thing for *Reader's Digest*. He likes to cut out the cartoons and make collages.

I wonder about Kim. There's no school today. I probably won't be in school tomorrow. She'll probably think I'm absent because I stayed out late listening to Adam and Shooting Star in Portland.

Portland. I am fairly certain that I'm being taken there. The helicopter pilot keeps talking to Trauma One. Outside the window, I can see the peak of Mount Hood looming. That means Portland is close.

Is Adam already there? He played in Seattle last night but he's always so full of adrenaline after a gig, and driving helps him to come down. The band is normally happy to let him chauffeur while they nap. If he's already in Portland, he's probably still asleep. When he wakes up, will he have coffee on

Hawthorne? Maybe take a book over to the Japanese Garden? That's what we did the last time I went to Portland with him, only it was warmer then. Later this afternoon, I know that the band will do a sound check. And then Adam will go outside to await my arrival. At first, he'll think that I'm late. How is he going to know that I'm actually early? That I got to Portland this morning while the snow was still melting?

"Have you ever heard of this Yo-Yo Ma dude?" Adam asked me. It was the spring of my sophomore year, which was his junior year. By then, Adam had been watching me practice in the music wing for several months. Our school was public, but one of those progressive ones that always got written up in national magazines because of its emphasis on the arts. We did get a lot of free periods to paint in the studio or practice music. I spent mine in the soundproof booths of the music wing. Adam was there a lot, too, playing guitar. Not the electric guitar he played in his band. Just acoustic melodies.

I rolled my eyes. "Everyone's heard of Yo-Yo Ma."

Adam grinned. I noticed for the first time that his smile was lopsided, his mouth sloping up on one side. He hooked his ringed thumb out toward the quad. "I don't think you'll find five people out there who've heard of Yo-Yo Ma. And by the way, what kind of name is that? Is it ghetto or something? Yo Mama?"

"It's Chinese."

Adam shook his head and laughed. "I know plenty of Chinese people. They have names like Wei Chin. Or Lee something. Not Yo-Yo Ma."

"You cannot be blaspheming the master," I said. But then I laughed in spite of myself. It had taken me a few months to believe that Adam wasn't taking the piss out of me, and after that we'd started having these little conversations in the corridor.

Still, his attention baffled me. It wasn't that Adam was such a popular guy. He wasn't a jock or a most-likely-to-succeed sort. But he was cool. Cool in that he played in a band with people who went to the college in town. Cool in that he had his own rockery style, procured from thrift stores and garage sales, not from Urban Outfitters knockoffs. Cool in that he seemed totally happy to sit in the lunchroom absorbed in a book, not just pretending to read because he didn't have anywhere to sit or anyone to sit with. That wasn't the case at all. He had a small group of friends and a large group of admirers.

And it wasn't like I was a dork, either. I had friends and a best friend to sit with at lunch. I had other good friends at the music conservatory camp I went to in the summer. People liked me well enough, but they also didn't really know me. I was quiet in class. I didn't raise my hand a lot or sass the teachers. And I was busy, much of my time spent practicing or playing in a string quartet or taking theory classes at the community college. Kids were nice enough to me, but they tended to treat me as if I were a grown-up. Another teacher. And you don't flirt with your teachers.

"What would you say if I said I had tickets to the master?" Adam asked me, a glint in his eyes.

"Shut up. You do not," I said, shoving him a little harder than I'd meant to.

Adam pretended to fall against the glass wall. Then he dusted himself off. "I do. At the Schnitzle place in Portland."

"It's the Arlene Schnitzer Hall. It's part of the Symphony."

"That's the place. I got tickets. A pair. You interested?"

"Are you serious? Yes! I was dying to go but they're like eighty dollars each. Wait, how did you get tickets?"

"A friend of the family gave them to my parents, but they can't go. It's no big thing," Adam said quickly. "Anyhow, it's Friday night. If you want, I'll pick you up at five-thirty and we'll drive to Portland together."

"Okay," I said, like it was the most natural thing.

By Friday afternoon, though, I was more jittery than when I'd inadvertently drunk a whole pot of Dad's tar-strong coffee while studying for finals last winter.

It wasn't Adam making me nervous. I'd grown comfortable enough around him by now. It was the uncertainty. What was this, exactly? A date? A friendly favor? An act of charity? I didn't like being on soft ground any more than I liked fumbling my way through a new movement. That's why I practiced so much, so I could rush myself on solid ground and then work out the details from there.

I changed my clothes about six times. Teddy, a kindergartner back then, sat in my bedroom, pulling the Calvin and Hobbes books down from the shelves and pretending to read them. He cracked himself up, though I wasn't sure whether it was Calvin's high jinks or my own making him so goofy.

Mom popped her head in to check on my progress. "He's just a guy, Mia," she said when she saw me getting worked up.

"Yeah, but he's just the first guy I've ever gone on a maybe-date with," I said. "So I don't know whether to wear date clothes or symphony clothes—do people here even dress up for that kind of thing? Or should I just keep it casual, in case it's *not* a date?"

"Just wear something you feel good in," she suggested. "That way you're covered." I'm sure Mom would've pulled out all the stops had she been me. In the pictures of her and Dad from the early days, she looked like a cross between a 1930s siren and a biker chick, with her pixie haircut, her big blue eyes coated in kohl eyeliner, and her rail-thin body always ensconced in some sexy getup, like a lacy vintage camisole paired with skintight leather pants.

I sighed. I wished I could be so ballsy. In the end, I chose a long black skirt and a maroon short-sleeved sweater. Plain and simple. My trademark, I guess.

When Adam showed up in a sharkskin suit and Creepers (an ensemble that wholly impressed Dad), I realized that this really *was* a date. Of course, Adam would choose to dress up for the symphony and a 1960s sharkskin suit could've just been his cool take on formal, but I knew there was more to it than that. He seemed nervous as he shook hands with my dad and told him that he had his band's old CDs. "To use as coasters, I hope," Dad said. Adam looked surprised, unused to the parent being more sarcastic than the child, I imagine.

"Don't you kids get too crazy. Bad injuries at the last Yo-Yo Ma mosh pit," Mom called as we walked down the lawn.

"Your parents are so cool," Adam said, opening the car door for me.

"I know," I replied.

We drove to Portland, making small talk. Adam played me snippets of bands he liked, a Swedish pop trio that sounded monotonous but then some Icelandic art band that was quite beautiful. We got a little lost downtown and made it to the concert hall with only a few minutes to spare.

Our seats were in the balcony. Nosebleeds. But you don't go to Yo-Yo Ma for the view, and the sound was incredible. That man has a way of making the cello sound like a crying woman one minute, a laughing child the next. Listening to him, I'm always reminded of why I started playing cello in the first place—that there is something so human and expressive about it.

When the concert started, I peered at Adam out of the corner of my eye. He seemed good-natured enough about the whole thing, but he kept looking at his program, probably counting off the movements until intermission. I worried that he was bored, but after a while I got too caught up in the music to care.

Then, when Yo-Yo Ma played "Le Grand Tango," Adam reached over and grasped my hand. In any other context, this would have been cheesy, the old yawn-and-cop-a-feel move. But Adam wasn't looking at me. His eyes were closed and he was swaying slightly in his seat. He was lost in the music, too. I squeezed his hand back and we sat there like that for the rest of the concert.

Afterward, we bought coffees and doughnuts and walked along the river. It was misting and he took off his suit jacket and draped it over my shoulders.

"You didn't really get those tickets from a family friend, did you?" I asked.

I thought he would laugh or throw up his arm in mock surrender like he did when I beat him in an argument. But he looked straight at me, so I could see the green and browns and grays swimming around in his irises. He shook his head. "That was two weeks of pizza-delivery tips," he admitted.

I stopped walking. I could hear the water lapping below. "Why?" I asked. "Why me?"

"I've never seen anyone get as into music as you do. It's why I like to watch you practice. You get the cutest crease in your forehead, right there," Adam said, touching me above the bridge of my nose. "I'm obsessed with music and even I don't get transported like you do."

"So, what? I'm like a social experiment to you?" I meant it to be jokey, but it came out sounding bitter.

"No, you're not an experiment," Adam said. His voice was husky and choked.

I felt the heat flood my neck and I could sense myself blushing. I stared at my shoes. I knew that Adam was looking at me now with as much certainty as I knew that if I looked up he was going to kiss me. And it took me by surprise how much I wanted to be kissed by him, to realize that I'd thought about it so often that I'd memorized the exact shape of his lips, that I'd imagined running my finger down the cleft of his chin.

My eyes flickered upward. Adam was there waiting for me.

That was how it started.

12:19 P.M.

There are a lot of things wrong with me.

Apparently, I have a collapsed lung. A ruptured spleen. Internal bleeding of unknown origin. And most serious, the contusions on my brain. I've also got broken ribs. Abrasions on my legs, which will require skin grafts; and on my face, which will require cosmetic surgery—but, as the doctors note, that is only if I am lucky.

Right now, in surgery, the doctors have to remove my spleen, insert a new tube to drain my collapsed lung, and stanch whatever else might be causing the internal bleeding. There isn't a lot they can do for my brain.

"We'll just wait and see," one of the surgeons says, looking at the CAT scan of my head. "In the meantime, call down to the blood bank. I need two units of O neg and keep two units ahead."

O negative. My blood type. I had no idea. It's not

like it's something I've ever had to think about before. I've never been in the hospital unless you count the time I went to the emergency room after I cut my ankle on some broken glass. I didn't even need stitches then, just a tetanus shot.

In the operating room, the doctors are debating what music to play, just like we were in the car this morning. One guy wants jazz. Another wants rock. The anesthesiologist, who stands near my head, requests classical. I root for her, and I feel like that must help because someone pops on a Wagner CD, although I don't know that the rousing "Ride of the Valkyries" is what I had in mind. I'd hoped for something a little lighter. *Four Seasons*, perhaps.

The operating room is small and crowded, full of blindingly bright lights, which highlight how grubby this place is. It's nothing like on TV, where operating rooms are like pristine theaters that could accommodate an opera singer, *and* an audience. The floor, though buffed shiny, is dingy with scuff marks and rust streaks, which I take to be old bloodstains.

Blood. It is everywhere. It does not faze the doctors one bit. They slice and sew and suction through a river of it, like they are washing dishes in soapy water. Meanwhile, they pump an ever-replenishing stock into my veins.

The surgeon who wanted to listen to rock sweats a lot. One of the nurses has to periodically dab him with gauze that she holds in tongs. At one point, he sweats through his mask and has to replace it.

The anesthesiologist has gentle fingers. She sits at my head, keeping an eye on all my vitals, adjusting the amounts of the fluids and gases and drugs they're giving me. She must be doing a good job because I don't appear to feel anything, even though they are yanking at my body. It's rough and messy work, nothing like that game Operation we used to play as kids where you had to be careful not to touch the sides as you removed a bone, or the buzzer would go off.

The anesthesiologist absentmindedly strokes my temples through her latex gloves. This is what Mom used to do when I came down with the flu or got one of those headaches that hurt so bad I used to imagine cutting open a vein in my temple just to relieve the pressure.

The Wagner CD has repeated twice now. The doctors decide it's time for a new genre. Jazz wins. People always assume that because I am into classical music, I'm a jazz aficionado. I'm not. Dad is.

He loves it, especially the wild, latter-day Coltrane stuff. He says that jazz is punk for old people. I guess that explains it, because I don't like punk, either.

The operation goes on and on. I'm exhausted by it. I don't know how the doctors have the stamina to keep up. They're standing still, but it seems harder than running a marathon.

I start to zone out. And then I start to wonder about this state I'm in. If I'm not dead—and the heart monitor is bleeping along, so I assume I'm not—but I'm not in my body, either, can I go anywhere? Am I a ghost? Could I transport myself to a beach in Hawaii? Can I pop over to Carnegie Hall in New York City? Can I go to Teddy?

Just for the sake of experiment, I wiggle my nose like Samantha on *Bewitched*. Nothing happens. I snap my fingers. Click my heels. I'm still here.

I decide to try a simpler maneuver. I walk into the wall, imagining that I'll float through it and come out the other side. Except that what happens when I walk into the wall is that I hit a wall.

A nurse bustles in with a bag of blood, and before the door shuts behind her, I slip through it. Now I'm in the hospital corridor. There are lots of doctors and nurses in blue and green scrubs hustling around. A woman on a gurney, her hair in a gauzy blue shower cap, an IV in her arm, calls out, "William, William." I walk a little farther. There are rows of operating rooms, all full of sleeping people. If the patients inside these rooms are like me, why then can't I see the people outside the people? Is everyone else loitering about like I seem to be? I'd really like to meet someone in my condition. I have some questions, like, what is this state I'm in exactly and how do I get out of it? How do I get back to my body? Do I have to wait for the doctors to wake me up? But there's no one else like me around. Maybe the rest of them figured out how to get to Hawaii.

I follow a nurse through a set of automatic double doors. I'm in a small waiting room now. My grandparents are here.

Gran is chattering away to Gramps, or maybe just to the air. It's her way of not letting emotion get the best of her. I've seen her do it before, when Gramps had a heart attack. She is wearing her Wellies and her gardening smock, which is smudged with mud. She must have been working in her greenhouse when she heard about us. Gran's hair is short and curly and gray; she's been wearing it in a permanent wave, Dad says, since the 1970s. "It's easy,"

Gran says. "No muss, no fuss." This is so typical of her. No nonsense. She's so quintessentially practical that most people would never guess she has a thing for angels. She keeps a collection of ceramic angels, yarn-doll angels, blown-glass angels, you-name-it angels, in a special china hutch in her sewing room. And she doesn't just collect angels; she believes in them. She thinks that they're everywhere. Once, a pair of loons nested in the pond in the woods behind their house. Gran was convinced that it was her long-dead parents, come to watch over her.

Another time, we were sitting outside on her porch and I saw a red bird. "Is that a red crossbill?" I'd asked Gran.

She'd shaken her head. "My sister Gloria is a crossbill," Gran had said, referring to my recently deceased great-aunt Glo, with whom Gran had never gotten along. "She wouldn't be coming around here."

Gramps is staring into the dregs of his Styrofoam cup, peeling away the top of it so that little white balls collect in his lap. I can tell it's the worst kind of swill, the kind that looks like it was brewed in 1997 and has been sitting on a burner ever since. Even so, I wouldn't mind a cup.

You can draw a straight line from Gramps to Dad

to Teddy, although Gramps's wavy hair has gone from blond to gray and he is stockier than Teddy, who is a stick, and Dad, who is wiry and muscular from afternoon weight-lifting sessions at the Y. But they all have the same watery gray-blue eyes, the color of the ocean on a cloudy day.

Maybe this is why I now find it hard to look at Gramps.

Juilliard was Gran's idea. She's from Massachusetts originally, but she moved to Oregon in 1955, on her own. Now that would be no big deal, but I guess fifty-two years ago it was kind of scandalous for a twenty-two-year-old unmarried woman to do that kind of thing. Gran claimed she was drawn to wild open wilderness and it didn't get more wild than the endless forests and craggy beaches of Oregon. She got a job as a secretary working for the Forest Service. Gramps was working there as a biologist.

We go back to Massachusetts sometimes in the summers, to a lodge in the western part of the state that for one week is taken over by Gran's extended family. That's when I see the second cousins and great aunts and uncles whose names I barely recognize. I have lots of family in Oregon, but they're all from Gramps's side.

Last summer at the Massachusetts retreat, I brought my cello so I could keep up my practicing for an upcoming chamber-music concert. The flight wasn't full, so the stewardesses let it travel in a seat next to me, just like the pros do it. Teddy thought this was hilarious and kept trying to feed it pretzels.

At the lodge, I gave a little concert one night, in the main room, with my relatives and the dead game animals mounted on the wall as my audience. It was after that that someone mentioned Juilliard, and Gran became taken with the idea.

At first, it seemed far-fetched. There was a perfectly good music program at the university near us. And, if I wanted to stretch, there was a conservatory in Seattle, which was only a few hours' drive. Juilliard was across the country. And expensive. Mom and Dad were intrigued with the idea of it, but I could tell neither one of them really wanted to relinquish me to New York City or go into hock so that I could maybe become a cellist for some second-rate small-town orchestra. They had no idea whether I was good enough. In fact, neither did I. Professor Christie told me that I was one of the most promising students she'd ever taught, but she'd never mentioned Juilliard to me. Juilliard was for virtuoso musicians, and it seemed arrogant to even think that they'd give me a second glance.

But after the retreat, when someone else, someone impartial and from the East Coast, deemed me Juilliard worthy, the idea burrowed into Gran's brain. She took it upon herself to speak to Professor Christie about it, and my teacher took hold of the idea like a terrier to a bone.

So, I filled out my application, collected my letters of recommendation, and sent in a recording of my playing. I didn't tell Adam about any of this. I had told myself that it was because there was no point advertising it when even getting an audition was such a long shot. But even then I'd recognized that for the lie that it was. A small part of me felt like even applying was some kind of betrayal. Juilliard was in New York. Adam was here.

But not at high school anymore. He was a year ahead of me, and this past year, my senior year, he'd started at the university in town. He only went to school part-time now because Shooting Star was starting to get popular. There was a record deal with a Seattle-based label, and a lot of traveling to gigs. So only after I got the creamy envelope embossed with *The Juilliard School* and a letter inviting me to audition did I tell Adam that I'd applied. I explained how many people didn't get that far. At first he looked a little awestruck, like he couldn't quite believe it. Then he gave a sad little smile. "Yo Mama better watch his back," he said.

The auditions were held in San Francisco. Dad had some big conference at the school that week and couldn't get away, and Mom had just started a new job at the travel agency, so Gran volunteered to accompany me. "We'll make a girls' weekend of it. Take high tea at the Fairmont. Go window-shopping in Union Square. Ride the ferry to Alcatraz. We'll be tourists."

But a week before we were due to leave, Gran tripped over a tree root and sprained her ankle. She had to wear one of those clunky boots and wasn't supposed to walk. Minor panic ensued. I said I could just go by myself—drive, or take the train, and come right back.

It was Gramps who insisted on taking me. We drove down together in his pickup truck. We didn't talk much, which was fine by me because I was so nervous. I kept fingering the Popsicle-stick good-luck talisman Teddy had presented me with before we left. "Break an arm," he'd told me.

Gramps and I listened to classical music and farm reports on the radio when we could pick up a station. Otherwise, we sat in silence. But it was such a calming silence; it made me relax and feel closer to him than any heart-to-heart would have.

Gran had booked us in a really frilly inn, and it was funny to see Gramps in his work boots and plaid flannel amid all the lacy doilies and potpourri. But he took it all in stride.

The audition was grueling. I had to play five pieces: a Shostakovich concerto, two Bach suites, all Tchaikovsky's *Pezzo capriccioso*, which was next to impossible, and a movement from Ennio Morricone's *The Mission*, a fun but risky choice because Yo-Yo Ma had covered this and everyone would compare. I walked out with my legs wobbly and my underarms wet with sweat. But my endorphins were surging and that, combined with the huge sense of relief, left me totally giddy.

"Shall we see the town?" Gramps asked, his lips twitching into a smile.

"Definitely!"

We did all the things Gran had promised we

would do. Gramps took me to high tea and shopping, although for dinner, we skipped out on the reservations Gran had made at some fancy place on Fisherman's Wharf and instead wandered into Chinatown, looking for the restaurant with the longest line of people waiting outside, and ate there.

When we got back home, Gramps dropped me off and enveloped me in a hug. Normally, he was a handshaker, maybe a back-patter on really special occasions. His hug was strong and tight, and I knew it was his way of telling me that he'd had a wonderful time.

"Me, too, Gramps," I whispered.

3:47 P.M.

They just moved me out of the recovery room into the trauma intensive-care unit, or ICU. It's a horseshoe-shaped room with about a dozen beds and a cadre of nurses, who constantly bustle around, reading the computer printouts that churn out from the feet of our beds recording our vital signs. In the middle of the room are more computers and a big desk, where another nurse sits.

I have two nurses who check in on me, along

with the endless round of doctors. One is a taciturn doughy man with blond hair and a mustache, who I don't much like. And the other is a woman with skin so black it's blue and a lilt in her voice. She calls me "sweetheart" and perpetually straightens the blankets around me, even though it's not like I'm kicking them off.

There are so many tubes attached to me that I cannot count them all: one down my throat breathing for me; one down my nose, keeping my stomach empty; one in my vein, hydrating me; one in my bladder, peeing for me; several on my chest, recording my heartbeat; another on my finger, recording my pulse. The ventilator that's doing my breathing has a soothing rhythm like a metronome, in, out, in, out.

No one, aside from the doctors and nurses and a social worker, has been in to see me. It's the social worker who speaks to Gran and Gramps in hushed sympathetic tones. She tells them that I am in "grave" condition. I'm not entirely sure what that means—grave. On TV, patients are always critical, or stable. Grave sounds bad. Grave is where you go when things don't work out here.

"I wish there was something we could do," Gran says. "I feel so useless just waiting."

"I'll see if I can get you in to see her in a little while," the social worker says. She has frizzy gray hair and a coffee stain on her blouse; her face is kind. "She's still sedated from the surgery and she's on a ventilator to help her breathe while her body heals from the trauma. But it can be helpful even for patients in a comatose state to hear from their loved ones."

Gramps grunts in reply.

"Do you have any people you can call?" the social worker asks. "Relatives who might like to be here with you. I understand this must be quite a trial for you, but the stronger you can be, the more it will help Mia."

I startle when I hear the social worker say my name. It's a jarring reminder that it's me they're talking about. Gran tells her about the various people who are en route right now, aunts, uncles. I don't hear any mention of Adam.

Adam is the one I really want to see. I wish I knew where he was so I could try to go there. I have no idea how he's going to find out about me. Gran and Gramps don't have his phone number. They don't carry cell phones, so he can't call them. And I don't know how he'd even know to call them. The people who would normally pass along pertinent information that something has happened to me are in no position to do that.

I stand over the bleeping tubed lifeless form that is me. My skin is gray. My eyes are taped shut. I wish someone would take the tape off. It looks like it itches. The nice nurse bustles over. Her scrubs have lollipops on them, even though this isn't a pediatric unit. "How's it going, sweetheart?" she asks me, as if we just bumped into each other in the grocery store.

It didn't start out so smoothly with Adam and me. I think I had this notion that love conquers all. And by the time he dropped me off from the Yo-Yo Ma concert, I think we were both aware that we were falling in love. I thought that getting to this part was the challenge. In books and movies, the stories always end when the two people finally have their romantic kiss. The happily-ever-after part is just assumed.

It didn't quite work that way for us. It turned out that coming from such far corners of the social universe had its downsides. We continued to see each other in the music wing, but these interactions remained platonic, as if neither one of us wanted to mess with a good thing. But whenever we met at other places in the school—when we sat together in the cafeteria or studied side by side on the quad on a sunny day—something was off. We were uncomfortable. Conversation was stilted. One of us would say something and the other would start to say something else at the same time.

"You go," I'd say.

"No, you go," Adam would say.

The politeness was painful. I wanted to push through it, to return to the glow of the night of the concert, but I was unsure of how to get back there.

Adam invited me to see his band play. This was even worse than school. If I felt like a fish out of water in my family, I felt like a fish on Mars in Adam's circle. He was always surrounded by funky, lively people, by cute girls with dyed hair and piercings, by aloof guys who perked up when Adam rock-talked with them. I couldn't do the groupie thing. And I didn't know how to rock-talk at all. It was a language I should've understood, being both a musician and Dad's daughter, but I didn't. It was like how Mandarin speakers can sort of understand Cantonese but not really, even though non-Chinese people assume all Chinese can communicate with one another, even though Mandarin and Cantonese are actually different.

I dreaded going to shows with Adam. It wasn't

that I was jealous. Or that I wasn't into his kind of music. I loved to watch him play. When he was onstage, it was like the guitar was a fifth limb, a natural extension of his body. And when he came offstage afterward, he would be sweaty but it was such a clean sweat that part of me was tempted to lick the side of his face, like it was a lollipop. I didn't, though.

Once the fans would descend, I'd skitter off to the sidelines. Adam would try to draw me back, to wrap an arm around my waist, but I'd disentangle myself and head back to the shadows.

"Don't you like me anymore?" Adam chided me after one show. He was kidding, but I could hear the hurt behind the offhand question.

"I don't know if I should keep coming to your shows," I said.

"Why not?" he asked. This time he didn't try to disguise the hurt.

"I feel like I keep you from basking in it all. I don't want you to have to worry about me."

Adam said that he didn't mind worrying about me, but I could tell that part of him did.

We probably would've broken up in those early weeks were it not for my house. At my house, with my family, we found a common ground. After we'd been together for a month, I took Adam home with me for his first family dinner with us. He sat in the kitchen with Dad, rock-talking. I observed, and I still didn't understand half of it, but unlike at the shows I didn't feel left out.

"Do you play basketball?" Dad asked. When it came to observing sports, Dad was a baseball fanatic, but when it came to playing, he loved to shoot hoops.

"Sure," Adam said. "I mean, I'm not very good."

"You don't need to be good; you just need to be committed. Want to play a quick game? You already have your basketball shoes on," Dad said, looking at Adam's Converse high-tops. Then he turned to me. "You mind?"

"Not at all," I said, smiling. "I can practice while you play."

They went out to the courts behind the nearby elementary school. They returned forty-five minutes later. Adam was covered with a sheen of sweat and looking a little dazed.

"What happened?" I asked. "Did the old man whoop you?"

Adam shook his head and nodded at the same time. "Well, yes. But it's not that. I got stung by a bee on my palm while we were playing. Your dad grabbed my hand and sucked the venom out."

I nodded. This was a trick he'd learned from Gran, and unlike with rattlesnakes, it actually worked on bee stings. You got the stinger and the venom out, so you were left with only a little itch.

Adam broke into an embarrassed smile. He leaned in and whispered into my ear: "I think I'm a little wigged out that I've been more intimate with your dad than I have with you."

I laughed at that. But it was sort of true. In the few weeks we'd been together, we hadn't done much more than kiss. It wasn't that I was a prude. I *was* a virgin, but I certainly wasn't devoted to staying that way. And Adam certainly wasn't a virgin. It was more that our kissing had suffered from the same painful politeness as our conversations.

"Maybe we should remedy that," I murmured.

Adam raised his eyebrows as if asking me a question. I blushed in response. All through dinner, we grinned at each other as we listened to Teddy, who was chattering about the dinosaur bones he'd apparently dug up in the back garden that afternoon. Dad had made his famous salt roast, which was my favorite dish, but I had no appetite. I pushed the food around my plate, hoping no one would notice. All the while, this little buzz was building inside me. I thought of the tuning fork I used to adjust my cello. Hitting it sets off vibrations in the note of A—vibrations that keep growing, and growing, until the harmonic pitch fills up the room. That's what Adam's grin was doing to me during dinner.

After the meal, Adam took a quick peek at Teddy's fossil finds, and then we went upstairs to my room and closed the door. Kim is not allowed to be alone in her house with boys—not that the opportunity ever came up. My parents had never mentioned any rules on this issue, but I had a feeling that they knew what was happening with Adam and me, and even though Dad liked to play it all *Father Knows Best*, in reality, he and Mom were suckers when it came to love.

Adam lay down on my bed, stretching his arms above his head. His whole face was grinning—eyes, nose, mouth. "Play me," he said.

"What?"

"I want you to play me like a cello."

I started to protest that this made no sense, but then I realized it made perfect sense. I went to my closet and grabbed one of my spare bows. "Take off your shirt," I said, my voice quavering.

Adam did. As thin as he was, he was surprisingly built. I could've spent twenty minutes staring at the contours and valleys of his chest. But he wanted me closer. *I* wanted me closer.

I sat down next to him on the bed so his long body was stretched out in front of me. The bow trembled as I placed it on the bed. I reached with my left hand and caressed Adam's head as if it were the scroll of my cello. He smiled again and closed his eyes. I relaxed a little. I fiddled with his ears as though they were the string pegs and then I playfully tickled him as he laughed softly. I placed two fingers on his Adam's apple. Then, taking a deep breath for courage, I plunged into his chest. I ran my hands up and down the length of his torso, focusing on the sinews in his muscles, assigning each one a string—A, G, C, D. I traced them down, one at a time, with the tip of my fingers. Adam got quiet then, as if he were concentrating on something.

I reached for the bow and brushed it across his hips, where I imagined the bridge of the cello would be. I played lightly at first and then with more force and speed as the song now playing in my head increased in intensity. Adam lay perfectly still, little groans escaping from his lips. I looked at the bow, looked at my hands, looked at Adam's face, and felt this surge of love, lust, and an unfamiliar feeling of power. I had never known that *I* could make someone feel this way.

When I finished, he stood up and kissed me long and deep. "My turn," he said. He pulled me to my feet and started by slipping the sweater over my head and edging down my jeans. Then he sat down on the bed and laid me across his lap. At first Adam did nothing except hold me. I closed my eyes and tried to feel his eyes on my body, seeing me as no one else ever had.

Then he began to play.

He strummed chords across the top of my chest, which tickled and made me laugh. He gently brushed his hands, moving farther down. I stopped giggling. The tuning fork intensified—its vibrations growing every time Adam touched me somewhere new.

After a while he switched to more of a Spanish-style, fingerpicking type of playing. He used the top of my body as the fret board, caressing my hair, my face, my neck. He plucked at my chest and my belly, but I could feel him in places his hands were nowhere near. As he played on, the energy magnified; the tuning fork going crazy now, firing off vibrations all over, until my entire body was humming, until I was left breathless. And when I felt like I could not take it one more minute, the swirl of sensations hit a dizzying crescendo, sending every nerve ending in my body on high alert.

I opened my eyes, savoring the warm calm that was sweeping over me. I started to laugh. Adam did, too. We kissed for a while longer until it was time for him to go home.

As I walked him out to his car, I wanted to tell him that I loved him. But it seemed like such a cliché after what we'd just done. So I waited and told him the next day. "That's a relief. I thought you might just be using me for sex," he joked, smiling.

After that, we still had our problems, but being overly polite with each other wasn't one of them.

4:39 P.M.

I have quite the crowd now. Gran and Gramps. Uncle Greg. Aunt Diane. Aunt Kate. My cousins Heather and John and David. Dad is one of five kids, so there are still lots more relatives out there.

Nobody is talking about Teddy, which leads me to believe that he's not here. He's probably still at the other hospital, being taken care of by Willow.

The relatives gather in the hospital waiting room. Not the little one on the surgical floor where Gran and Gramps were during my operation, but a larger one on the hospital's main floor that is tastefully decorated in shades of mauve and has comfy chairs and sofas and magazines that are almost current. Everyone still talks in hushed tones, as if being respectful of the other people waiting, even though it's only my family in the waiting room. It's all so serious, so ominous. I go back into the hallway to get a break.

I'm so happy when Kim arrives; happy to see the familiar sight of her long black hair in a single braid. She wears the braid every day and always, by lunchtime, the curls and ringlets of her thick mane have managed to escape in rebellious little tendrils. But she refuses to surrender to that hair of hers, and every morning, it goes back into the braid.

Kim's mother is with her. She doesn't let Kim drive long distances, and I guess that after what's happened, there's no way she'd make an exception today. Mrs. Schein is red-faced and blotchy, like she's been crying or is about to cry. I know this because I have seen her cry many times. She's very emotional. "Drama queen," is how Kim puts it. "It's the Jewish-mother gene. She can't help it. I suppose I'll be like that one day, too," Kim concedes.

Kim is so the opposite of that, so droll and funny in a low-key way that she's always having to say "just kidding" to people who don't get her sarcastic sense of humor, that I cannot imagine her ever being like her mother. Then again, I don't have much basis for comparison. There are not a lot of Jewish mothers in our town or that many Jewish kids at our school. And the kids who are Jewish are usually only half, so all it means is that they have a menorah alongside their Christmas trees.

But Kim is really Jewish. Sometimes I have Friday-night dinner with her family when they light candles, eat braided bread, and drink wine (the only time I can imagine neurotic Mrs. Schein allowing Kim to drink). Kim's expected to only date Jewish guys, which means she doesn't date. She jokes that this is the reason her family moved here, when in fact it was because her father was hired to run a computer-chip plant. When she was thirteen, she had a bat mitzvah at a temple in Portland, and during the candlelighting ceremony at the reception, I got called up to light one. Every summer, she goes to Jewish sleepaway camp in New Jersey. It's called Camp Torah Habonim, but Kim calls it *Torah Whore,* because all the kids do all summer is hook up.

"Just like band camp," she joked, though my summer conservatory program is nothing like *American Pie.*

Right now I can see Kim is annoyed. She's walking fast, keeping a good ten feet between her and her mother as they march down the halls. Suddenly her shoulders go up like a cat that's just spied a dog. She swerves to face her mother.

"Stop it!" Kim demands. "If I'm not crying, there's no fucking way you're allowed to."

Kim never curses. So this shocks me.

"But," Mrs. Schein protests, "how can you be so . . ."—sob—"so calm when—"

"Cut it out!" Kim interjects. "Mia is still here. So I'm not losing it. And if I don't lose it, you don't get to!"

Kim stalks off in the direction of the waiting room, her mother following limply behind. When they reach the waiting room and see my assembled family, Mrs. Schein starts sniffling.

Kim doesn't curse this time. But her ears go pink, which is how I know she's still furious. "Mother. I am going to leave you here. I'm taking a walk. I'll be back later."

I follow her back out into the corridor. She wanders around the main lobby, loops around the gift shop, visits the cafeteria. She looks at the hospital directory. I think I know where she's headed before she does.

There's a small chapel in the basement. It's hushed in there, a library kind of quiet. There are plush chairs like the kind you find at a movie theater, and a muted soundtrack playing some New Agey–type music.

Kim slumps back in one of the chairs. She takes off her coat, the one that is black and velvet and that I have coveted since she bought it at some mall in New Jersey on a trip to visit her grandparents.

"I love Oregon," she says with a hiccup attempt at a laugh. I can tell by her sarcastic tone that it's me she's talking to, not God. "This is the hospital's idea of nondenominational." She points around the chapel. There is a crucifix mounted on the wall, a flag of a cross draped over the lectern, and a few paintings of the Madonna and Child hanging in the back. "We have a token Star of David," she says, gesturing to the six-pointed star on the wall. "But what about the Muslims? No prayer rugs or symbol to show which way is east toward Mecca? And what about the Buddhists? Couldn't they spring for a gong? I mean there are probably more Buddhists than Jews in Portland anyway."

I sit down in a chair beside her. It feels so natural the way that Kim is talking to me like she always does. Other than the paramedic who told me to hang in there and the nurse who keeps asking me how I'm doing, no one has talked to me since the accident. They talk about me.

I've never actually seen Kim pray. I mean, she prayed at her bat mitzvah and she does the blessings at Shabbat dinner, but that is because she has to. Mostly, she makes light of her religion. But after she talks to me for a while, she closes her eyes and moves her lips and murmurs things in a language I don't understand.

She opens her eyes and wipes her hands together as if to say *enough of that*. Then she reconsiders and adds a final appeal. "Please don't die. I can understand why you'd want to, but think about this: If you die, there's going to be one of those cheesy Princess Diana memorials at school, where everyone puts flowers and candles and notes next to your locker." She wipes away a renegade tear with the back of her hand. "I know you'd hate that kind of thing."

⌇

Maybe it was because we were too alike. As soon as Kim showed up on the scene, everyone assumed we'd be best friends just because we were both dark, quiet, studious, and, at least outwardly, serious. The thing was, neither one of us was a particularly great student (straight B averages all around) or, for that matter, all that serious. We were serious about certain things—music in my case, art and photography in hers—and in the simplified world of middle school, that was enough to set us apart as separated twins of some sort.

Immediately we got shoved together for everything. On Kim's third day of school, she was the only person to volunteer to be a team captain during a soccer match in PE, which I'd thought was beyond suck-uppy of her. As she put on her red jersey, the coach scanned the class to pick Team B's captain, his eyes settling on me, even though I was one of the least athletic girls. As I shuffled over to put on my jersey, I brushed past Kim, mumbling "thanks a lot."

The following week, our English teacher paired us together for a joint oral discussion on *To Kill a Mockingbird*. We sat across from each other in stony silence for about ten minutes. Finally, I said. "I guess we should talk about racism in the Old South, or something."

Kim ever so slightly rolled her eyes, which made me want to throw a dictionary at her. I was caught off guard by how intensely I already hated her. "I read this book at my old school," she said. "The racism thing is kind of obvious. I think the bigger thing is people's goodness. Are they naturally good and turned bad by stuff like racism or are they naturally bad and need to work hard not to be?"

"Whatever," I said. "It's a stupid book." I didn't know why I'd said that because I'd actually loved the book and had talked to Dad about it; he was using it for his student teaching. I hated Kim even more for making me betray a book I loved.

"Fine. We'll do your idea, then," Kim said, and when we got a B minus, she seemed to gloat about our mediocre grade.

After that, we just didn't talk. That didn't stop teachers from pairing us together or everyone in the school from assuming that we were friends. The more that happened, the more we resented it—and each other. The more the world shoved us together, the more we shoved back—and against each other. We tried to pretend the other didn't exist even though the existence of our nemeses kept us both occupied for hours.

I felt compelled to give myself reasons why I hated Kim: She was a Goody Two-shoes. She was annoying. She was a show-off. Later, I found out that she did the same thing about me, though her major complaint was that she thought I was a bitch. And one day, she even wrote it to me. In English class, someone flung a folded-up square of note-book paper onto the floor next to my right foot. I picked it up and opened it. It read, *Bitch!*

Nobody had ever called me that before, and though I was automatically furious, deep down I was also flattered that I had elicited enough emotion to be worthy of the name. People called Mom that a lot, probably because she had a hard time holding her tongue and could be brutally blunt when she disagreed with you. She'd explode like a thunderstorm, and then be fine again. Anyhow, she didn't care that people called her a bitch. "It's just another word for feminist," she told me with pride. Even Dad called her that sometimes, but always in a jokey, complimentary way. Never during a fight. He knew better.

I looked up from my grammar book. There was only one person who would've sent this note to me, but I still scarcely believed it. I peered at the class. Everyone had their faces in their books. Except for Kim. Her ears were so red that it made the little sideburnlike tendrils of dark hair look like they were also blushing. She was glaring at me. I might have been eleven years old and a little socially immature, but I recognized a gauntlet being thrown down when I saw it, and I had no choice but to take it up.

When we got older, we liked to joke that we were so glad we had that fistfight. Not only did it cement our friendship but it also provided us our first and likely *only* opportunity for a good brawl. When else were two girls like us going to come to blows? I wrestled on the ground with Teddy, and sometimes I pinched him, but a fistfight? He was just a baby, and even if he were older, Teddy was like half kid brother and half my own kid. I'd been babysitting him since he was a few weeks old. I could never hurt him like that. And Kim, an only child, didn't have any siblings to sock. Maybe at camp she could've gotten into a scuffle, but the consequences would've been dire: hours-long conflict-resolution seminars with the counselors and the rabbi. "My people know how to fight with the best of them, but with words, with lots and lots of words," she told me once.

But that fall day, we fought with fists. After the last bell, without a word, we followed each other out to the playground, dropped our backpacks on the ground, which was wet from the day's steady drizzle. She charged me like a bull, knocking the wind out of me. I punched her on the side of the head, fist closed, like men do. A crowd of kids gathered around to witness the spectacle. Fighting was novelty enough at our school. Girl-fighting was extra special. And good girls going at it was like hitting the trifecta.

By the time teachers separated us, half of the sixth grade was watching us (in fact, it was the ring of students loitering that alerted the playground monitors that something was up). The fight was a tie, I suppose. I had a split lip and a bruised wrist, the latter inflicted upon myself when my swing at Kim's shoulder missed her and landed squarely on the pole of the volleyball net. Kim had a swollen eye and a bad scrape on her thigh as a result of her tripping over her backpack as she attempted to kick me.

There was no heartfelt peacemaking, no official détente. Once the teachers separated us, Kim and I looked at each other and started laughing. After finagling ourselves out of a visit to the principal's office, we limped home. Kim told me that the only reason that she volunteered for team captain was that if you did that at the beginning of a school year, coaches tended to remember and that actually kept them from picking you in the future (a handy trick I co-opted from then on). I explained to her that I actually agreed with her take on *To Kill a Mockingbird*, which was one of my favorite books. And then that was it. We were friends, just as everyone had assumed all along that we would be. We never laid a hand on each other again, and even though we'd get into plenty of verbal clashes, our tiffs tended to end the way our fistfight had, with us cracking up.

After our big brawl, though, Mrs. Schein refused to let Kim come over to my house, convinced that her daughter would return on crutches. Mom offered to go over and smooth things out, but I think that Dad and I both realized that given her temper, her diplomatic mission might end up with a restraining order against our family. In the end, Dad invited the Scheins over for a roast-chicken dinner, and though you could see Mrs. Schein was still a little weirded out by my family—"So you work in a record store while you study to become a teacher? And *you* do the cooking? How unusual," she said to Dad—Mr. Schein declared my parents decent and our family nonviolent and told Kim's mother that Kim ought to be allowed to come and go freely.

For those few months in sixth grade, Kim and I shed our good-girl personas. Talk about our fight circulated, the details growing more exaggerated—broken ribs, torn-off fingernails, bite marks. But when we came back to school after winter break, it was all forgotten. We were back to being the dark, quiet, good-girl twins.

We didn't mind anymore. In fact, over the years that reputation has served us well. If, for instance, we were both absent on the same day, people automatically assumed we had come down with the same bug, not that we'd ditched school to watch art films being shown in the film-survey class at the university. When, as a prank, someone put our school up for sale, covering it with signs and posting a listing on eBay, suspicious eyes turned to Nelson Baker and Jenna McLaughlin, not to us. Even if we had owned up to the prank—as we'd planned to if anyone else got in trouble—we'd have had a hard time convincing anyone it really was us.

This always made Kim laugh. "People believe what they want to believe," she said.

4:47 P.M.

Mom once snuck me into a casino. We were going on vacation to Crater Lake and we stopped at a resort on an Indian reservation for the buffet lunch. Mom decided to do a bit of gambling, and I went with her while Dad stayed with Teddy, who was napping in his stroller. Mom sat down at the dollar blackjack tables. The dealer looked at me, then at Mom, who returned his mildly suspicious glance with a look sharp enough to cut diamonds followed by a smile more brilliant that any gem. The dealer sheepishly smiled back and didn't say a word. I watched Mom play, mesmerized. It seemed like we were in there for fifteen minutes but then Dad and Teddy came in search of us, both of them grumpy. It turned out we'd been there for over an hour.

The ICU is like that. You can't tell what time of day it is or how much time has passed. There's no natural light. And there's a constant soundtrack of noise, only instead of the electronic beeping of slot machines and the satisfying jangle of quarters, it's the hum and whir of all the medical equipment, the endless muffled pages over the PA, and the steady talk of the nurses.

I'm not entirely sure how long I've been in here. A while ago, the nurse I liked with the lilting accent said she was going home. "I'll be back tomorrow, but I want to see you here, sweetheart," she said. I thought that was weird at first. Wouldn't she want me to be home, or moved to another part of the hospital? But then I realized that she meant she wanted to see me in this ward, as opposed to dead.

The doctors keep coming around and pulling up my eyelids and waving around a flashlight. They are rough and hurried, like they don't consider eyelids worthy of gentleness. It makes you realize how little in life we touch one another's eyes. Maybe your parents will hold an eyelid up to get out a piece of dirt, or maybe your boyfriend will kiss your eyelids, light as a butterfly, just before you drift off to sleep. But eyelids are not like elbows or knees or shoulders, parts of the body accustomed to being jostled.

The social worker is at my bedside now. She is looking through my chart and talking to one of the nurses who normally sits at the big desk in the middle of the room. It is amazing the ways they watch you here. If they're not waving penlights in your eyes or reading the printouts that come tumbling out from the bedside printers, then they are watching your vitals from a central computer screen. If anything goes slightly amiss, one of the monitors starts bleeping. There is always an alarm going off somewhere. At first, it scared me, but now I realize that half the time, when the alarms go off, it's the machines that are malfunctioning, not the people.

The social worker looks exhausted, as if she wouldn't mind crawling into one of the open beds. I am not her only sick person. She has been shuttling back and forth between patients and families all afternoon. She's the bridge between the doctors and the people, and you can see the strain of balancing between those two worlds.

After she reads my chart and talks to the nurses, she goes back downstairs to my family, who have stopped talking in hushed tones and are now all engaged in solitary activities. Gran is knitting. Gramps is pretending to nap. Aunt Diane playing sudoku. My cousins are taking turns on a Game Boy, the sound turned to mute.

Kim has left. When she came back to the waiting room after visiting the chapel, she found Mrs. Schein a total wreck. She seemed so embarrassed and she hustled her mother out. Actually, I think having Mrs. Schein there probably helped. Comforting her gave everyone else something to do, a way to feel useful. Now they're back to feeling useless, back to the endless wait.

When the social worker walks into the waiting room, everyone stands up, like they're greeting royalty. She gives a half smile, which I've seen her do several times already today. I think it's her signal that everything is okay, or status quo, and she's just here to deliver an update, not to drop a bomb.

"Mia is still unconscious, but her vital signs are improving," she tells the assembled relatives, who have abandoned their distractions haphazardly on the chairs. "She's in with the respiratory therapists right now. They're running tests to see how her lungs are functioning and whether she can be weaned off the ventilator."

"That's good news, then?" Aunt Diane asks. "I mean if she can breathe on her own, then she'll wake up soon?"

The social worker gives a practiced sympathetic nod. "It's a good step if she can breathe on her own.

It shows her lungs are healing and her internal injuries are stabilizing. The question mark is still the brain contusions."

"Why is that?" Cousin Heather interrupts.

"We don't know when she will wake up on her own, or the extent of the damage to her brain. These first twenty-four hours are the most critical and Mia is getting the best possible care."

"Can we see her?" Gramps asks.

The social worker nods. "That's why I'm here. I think it would be good for Mia to have a short visit. Just one or two people."

"We'll go," Gran says, stepping forward. Gramps is by her side.

"Yes, that's what I thought," the social worker says. "We won't be long," she says to the rest of the family.

The three of them walk down the hall in silence. In the elevator, the social worker attempts to prepare my grandparents for the sight of me, explaining the extent of my external injuries, which look bad, but are treatable. It's the internal injuries that they're worried about, she says.

She's acting like my grandparents are children. But they're tougher than they look. Gramps was a medic in Korea. And Gran, she's always rescuing things: birds with broken wings, a sick beaver, a deer hit by a car. The deer went to a wildlife sanctuary, which is funny because Gran usually hates deer; they eat up her garden. "Pretty rats," she calls them. "Tasty rats" is what Gramps calls them when he grills up venison steaks. But that one deer, Gran couldn't bear to see it suffer, so she rescued it. Part of me suspects she thought it was one of her angels.

Still, when they come through the automatic double doors into the ICU, both of them stop, as if repelled by an invisible barrier. Gran takes Gramps's hand, and I try to remember if I've ever seen them hold hands before. Gran scans the beds for me, but just as the social worker starts to point out where I am, Gramps sees me and he strides across the floor to my bed.

"Hello, duck," he says. He hasn't called me that in ages, not since I was younger than Teddy. Gran walks slowly to where I am, taking little gulps of air as she comes. Maybe those wounded animals weren't such good prep after all.

The social worker pulls over two chairs, setting them up at the foot of my bed. "Mia, your grandparents are here." She motions for them to sit down. "I'll leave you alone now."

"Can she hear us?" Gran asks. "If we talk to her, she'll understand?"

"Truly, I don't know," the social worker responds. "But your presence can be soothing so long as what you say is soothing." Then she gives them a stern look, as if to tell them not to say anything bad to upset me. I know it's her job to warn them about things like this and that she is busy with a thousand things and can't always be so sensitive, but for a second, I hate her.

After the social worker leaves, Gran and Gramps sit in silence for a minute. Then Gran starts prattling on about the orchids she's growing in her greenhouse. I notice that she's changed out of her gardening smock into a clean pair of corduroy pants and a sweater. Someone must have stopped by her house to bring her fresh clothes. Gramps is sitting very still, and his hands are shaking. He's not much of a talker, so it must be hard for him being ordered to chat with me now.

Another nurse comes by. She has dark hair and dark eyes brightened with lots of shimmery eye makeup. Her nails are acrylic and have heart decals on them. She must have to work hard to keep her nails so pretty. I admire that.

She's not my nurse but she comes up to Gran and Gramps just the same. "Don't you doubt for a second that she can hear you," she tells them. "She's aware of everything that's going on." She stands there with her hands on her hips. I can almost picture her snapping gum. Gran and Gramps stare at her, lapping up what she's telling them. "You might think that the doctors or nurses or all this is running the show," she says, gesturing to the wall of medical equipment. "Nuh-uh. *She's* running the show. Maybe she's just biding her time. So you talk to her. You tell her to take all the time she needs, but to come on back. You're waiting for her."

Mom and Dad would never call Teddy or me mistakes. Or accidents. Or surprises. Or any of those other stupid euphemisms. But neither one of us was planned, and they never tried to hide that.

Mom got pregnant with me when she was young. Not teenager-young, but young for their set of friends. She was twenty-three and she and Dad had already been married for a year.

In a funny way, Dad was always a bow-tie wearer, always a little more traditional than you might imagine. Because even though he had blue hair and tattoos and wore leather jackets and worked in a record store, he wanted to marry Mom back at a time when the rest of their friends were still having drunken one-night stands. "*Girlfriend* is such a stupid word," he said. "I couldn't stand calling her that. So, we had to get married, so I could call her 'wife.'"

Mom, for her part, had a messed-up family. She didn't go into the gory details with me, but I knew her father was long gone and for a while she had been out of touch with her mother, though now we saw Grandma and Papa Richard, which is what we called Mom's stepfather, a couple times a year.

So Mom was taken not just with Dad but with the big, mostly intact, relatively normal family he belonged to. She agreed to marry Dad even though they'd been together just a year. Of course, they still did it their way. They were married by a lesbian justice of the peace while their friends played a guitar-feedback-heavy version of the "Wedding March." The bride wore a white-fringed flapper dress and black spiked boots. The groom wore leather.

They got pregnant with me because of someone else's wedding. One of Dad's music buddies who'd moved to Seattle had gotten his girlfriend pregnant, so they were doing the shotgun thing. Mom and Dad went to the wedding, and at the reception, they got a little drunk and back at the hotel weren't as careful as usual. Three months later there was a thin blue line on the pregnancy test.

The way they tell it, neither felt particularly ready to be parents. Neither one felt like an adult yet. But there was no question that they would have me. Mom was adamantly pro-choice. She had a bumper sticker on the car that read *If you can't trust me with a choice, how can you trust me with a child?* But in her case the choice was to keep me.

Dad was more hesitant. More freaked out. Until the minute the doctor pulled me out and then he started to cry.

"That's poppycock," he would say when Mom recounted the story. "I did no such thing."

"You didn't cry then?" Mom asked in sarcastic amusement.

"I *teared*. I did not cry." Then Dad winked at me and pantomimed weeping like a baby.

Because I was the only kid in Mom and Dad's group of friends, I was a novelty. I was raised by the music community, with dozens of aunties and uncles who took me in as their own little foundling, even after I started showing a strange preference for classical music. I didn't want for real family, either. Gran and Gramps lived nearby, and they were happy to take me for weekends so Mom and Dad could act wild and stay out all night for one of Dad's shows.

Around the time I was four, I think my parents realized that they were actually doing it—raising a kid—even though they didn't have a ton of money or "real" jobs. We had a nice house with cheap rent. I had clothes (even if they were hand-me-downs from my cousins) and I was growing up happy and healthy. "You were like an experiment," Dad said. "Surprisingly successful. We thought it must be a fluke. We needed another kid as a kind of control group."

They tried for four years. Mom got pregnant twice and had two miscarriages. They were sad about it, but they didn't have the money to do all the fertility stuff that people do. By the time I was nine, they'd decided that maybe it was for the best. I was becoming independent. They stopped trying.

As if to convince themselves how great it was not to be tied down by a baby, Mom and Dad bought us tickets to go visit New York for a week. It was supposed to be a musical pilgrimage. We would go to CBGB's and Carnegie Hall. But when to her surprise, Mom discovered she was pregnant, and then to her greater surprise, stayed pregnant past the first trimester, we had to cancel the trip. She was tired and sick to her stomach and so grumpy Dad joked that she'd probably scare the New Yorkers. Besides, babies were expensive and we needed to save.

I didn't mind. I was excited about a baby. And I knew that Carnegie Hall wasn't going anywhere. I'd get there someday.

5:40 P.M.

I am a little freaked out right now. Gran and Gramps left a while ago, but I stayed behind here in the ICU. I am sitting in one the chairs, going over their conversation, which was very nice and normal and nondisturbing. Until they left. As Gran and Gramps walked out of the ICU, with me following, Gramps turned to Gran and asked: "Do you think she decides?"

"Decides what?"

Gramps looked uncomfortable. He shuffled his feet. "You know? Decides," he whispered.

"What are you talking about?" Gran sounded exasperated and tender at the same time.

"I don't know what I'm talking about. You're the one who believes in all the angels."

"What does that have to do with Mia?" Gran asked.

"If they're gone now, but still here, like you believe, what if they want her to join them? What if she wants to join them?"

"It doesn't work like that," Gran snapped.

"Oh," was all Gramps said. The inquiry was over.

After they left, I was thinking that one day maybe I'll tell Gran that I never much bought into her theory that birds and such could be people's guardian angels. And now I'm more sure than ever that there's no such thing.

My parents aren't here. They are not holding my hand, or cheering me on. I know them well enough to know that if they could, they would. Maybe not both of them. Maybe Mom would stay with Teddy while Dad watched over me. But neither of them is here.

And it's while contemplating this that I think about what the nurse said. *She's running the show.* And suddenly I understand what Gramps was really asking Gran. He had listened to that nurse, too. He got it before I did.

If I stay. If I live. It's up to me.

All this business about medically induced comas is just doctor talk. It's not up to the doctors. It's not up to the absentee angels. It's not even up to God who, if He exists, is nowhere around right now. It's up to me.

How am I supposed to decide this? How can I possibly stay without Mom and Dad? How can I leave without Teddy? Or Adam? This is too much. I don't even understand how it all works, why I'm here in the state that I'm in or how to get out of it if I wanted to. If I were to say, *I want to wake up,* would I wake up right now? I already tried snapping my heels to find Teddy and trying to beam myself to Hawaii, and that didn't work. This seems a whole lot more complicated.

But in spite of that, I believe it's true. I hear the nurse's words again. I am running the show. Everyone is waiting on me.

I decide. I know this now.

And this terrifies me more than anything else that has happened today.

Where the hell is Adam?

~~~

A week before Halloween of my junior year, Adam showed up at my door triumphant. He was holding a dress bag and wearing a shit-eating grin.

"Prepare to writhe in jealousy. I just got the best costume," he said. He unzipped the bag. Inside was a frilly white shirt, a pair of breeches, and a long wool coat with epaulets.

"You're going to be Seinfeld with the puffy shirt?" I asked.

"Pff. *Seinfeld*. And you call yourself a classical musician. I'm going to be Mozart. Wait, you haven't seen the shoes." He reached into the bag and pulled out clunky black leather numbers with metal bars across the tops.

"Nice," I said. "I think my mom has a pair like them."

"You're just jealous because you don't have such a rockin' costume. And I'll be wearing tights, too. I'm just that secure in my manhood. Also, I have a wig."

"Where'd you get all this?" I asked, fingering the wig. It felt like it was made of burlap.

"Online. Only a hundred bucks."

"You spent a hundred dollars on a Halloween costume?"

At the mention of the word *Halloween,* Teddy zoomed down the stairs, ignoring me and yanking on Adam's wallet chain. "Wait here!" he demanded, and then ran back upstairs and returned a few seconds later holding a bag. "Is this a good costume? Or will it make me look babyish?" Teddy asked, pulling out a pitchfork, a set of devil ears, a red tail, and a pair of red feetie pajamas.

"Ohh." Adam stepped backward, his eyes wide. "That outfit scares the hell out of me and you aren't even wearing it."

"Really? You don't think the pajamas make it look dumb. I don't want anyone to laugh at me," Teddy declared, his eyebrows furrowed in seriousness.

I grinned at Adam, who was trying to swallow his own smile. "Red pajamas plus pitchfork plus devil ears and pointy tail is so fully satanic no one would dare challenge you, lest they risk eternal damnation," Adam assured him.

Teddy's face broke into a wide grin, showing off the gap of his missing front tooth. "That's kind of what Mom said, but I just wanted to make sure she wasn't just telling me that so I wouldn't bug her about the costume. You're taking me trick-or-treating, right?" He looked at me now.

"Just like every year," I answered. "How else am I gonna get candy?"

"You're coming, too?" he asked Adam.

"I wouldn't miss it."

Teddy turned on his heel and whizzed back up the stairs. Adam turned to me. "That's Teddy settled. What are you wearing?"

"Ahh, I'm not much of a costume girl."

Adam rolled his eyes. "Well, become one. It's Halloween, our first one together. Shooting Star has a big show that night. It's a costume concert, and you promised to go."

Inwardly, I groaned. After six months with Adam, I had just gotten used to us being the odd couple at school—people called us Groovy and the Geek. And I was starting to become more comfortable with Adam's bandmates, and had even learned a few words of rock-talk. I could hold my own now when Adam took me to the House of Rock, the rambling house near the college where the rest of the band all lived. I could even participate in the band's punk-rock pot-luck parties when everyone invited had to bring something from their fridge that was on the verge of spoiling. We took all the ingredients and made something out of it. I was actually pretty good at finding ways to turn the vegetarian ground beef, beets, feta cheese, and apricots into something edible.

But I still hated the shows and hated myself for hating them. The clubs were smoky, which hurt my eyes and made my clothes stink. The speakers were always turned up so high that the music blared, causing my ears to ring so loudly afterward that the high-pitched drone would actually keep me up. I'd lie in bed, replaying the awkward night and feeling shittier about it with each playback.

"Don't tell me you're gonna back out," Adam said, looking equal parts hurt and irritated.

"What about Teddy? We promised we'd take him trick-or-treating—"

"Yeah, at five o'clock. We don't have to be at the show until ten. I doubt even Master Ted could trick-or-treat for five solid hours. So you have no excuse. And you'd better get a good outfit together because I'm going to look hot, in an eighteenth-century kind of way."

After Adam left to go to work delivering pizzas, I had a pit in my stomach. I went upstairs to practice the Dvořák piece Professor Christie had assigned me, and to work out what was bothering me. Why didn't I like his shows? Was it because Shooting Star was getting popular and I was jealous? Did the ever-growing masses of girl groupies put me off? This seemed like a logical enough explanation, but it wasn't it.

After I'd played for about ten minutes, it came to me: My aversion to Adam's shows had nothing to do with music or groupies or envy. It had to do with the doubts. The same niggling doubts I always had about not belonging. I didn't feel like I belonged with my family, and now I didn't feel like I belonged with Adam, except unlike my family, who was stuck with me, Adam had chosen me, and this I didn't understand. Why had he fallen for *me*? It didn't make sense. I knew it was music that brought us together in the first place, put us in the same space so we could even get to know each other. And I knew that Adam liked how into music I was. And that he dug my sense of humor, "so dark you almost miss it," he said. And, speaking of dark, I knew he had a thing for dark-haired girls because all of his girlfriends had been brunettes. And I knew that when it was the two of us alone together, we could talk for hours, or sit reading side by side for hours, each one plugged into our own iPod, and still feel completely together. I understood all that in my head, but I still didn't believe it in my heart. When I was with Adam, I felt picked, chosen, special, and that just made me wonder *why me?* even more.

And maybe this was why even though Adam willingly submitted to Schubert symphonies and attended any recital I gave, bringing me stargazer lilies, my favorite flower, I'd still rather have gone to the dentist than to one of his shows. Which was so churlish of me. I thought of what Mom sometimes said to me when I was feeling insecure: "Fake it till you make it." By the time I finished playing the piece three times over, I decided that not only would I go to his show, but for once I'd make as much of an effort to understand his world as he did mine.

"I need your help," I told Mom that night after dinner as we stood side by side doing dishes.

"I think we've established that I'm not very good at trigonometry. Maybe you can try the online-tutor thing," Mom said.

"Not math help. Something else."

"I'll do my best. What do you need?"

"Advice. Who's the coolest, toughest, hottest rocker girl you can think of?"

"Debbie Harry," Mom said.

"Tha—"

"Not finished," Mom interrupted. "You can't ask me to pick only one. That's so *Sophie's Choice*. Kathleen Hanna. Patti Smith. Joan Jett. Courtney Love, in her demented destructionist way. Lucinda Williams, even though she's country she's tough as nails. Kim Gordon from Sonic Youth, pushing fifty and still at it. That Cat Power woman. Joan Armatrading. Why, is this some kind of social-studies project?"

"Kind of," I answered, toweling off a chipped plate. "It's for Halloween."

Mom clapped her soapy hands together in delight. "You planning on impersonating one of us?"

"Yeah," I replied. "Can you help me?"

Mom took off work early so we could trawl through vintage-clothing stores. She decided we should go for a pastiche of rocker looks, rather than trying to copy any one artist. We bought a pair of tight, lizard-skin pants. A blond bobbed wig with severe bangs, à la early-eighties Debbie Harry, which Mom streaked with purple Manic Panic. For accessories, we got a black leather band for one wrist and about two dozen silver bangles for the other. Mom fished out a her own vintage Sonic Youth T-shirt—warning me not to take it off lest someone grab it and sell it on eBay for a couple hundred bucks—and the pair of black, pointy-toed leather spiked boots that she'd worn to her wedding.

On Halloween, she did my makeup, thick streaks of black liquid eyeliner that made my eyes look dangerous. White powder that made my skin pale. Bloodred gashes on my lips. A stick-on nose ring. When I looked in the mirror, I saw Mom's face peering back at me. Maybe it was the blond wig, but this was the first time I ever thought I actually looked like any of my immediate family.

My parents and Teddy waited downstairs for Adam while I stayed in my room. It felt like this was prom or something. Dad held the camera. Mom was practically dancing with excitement. When Adam came through door, showering Teddy with Skittles, Mom and Dad called me down.

I did a slinky walk as best as I could in the heels. I'd expected Adam to go crazy when he saw me, his jeans-and-sweaters girlfriend all glammed out. But he smiled his usual greeting, chuckling a bit. "Nice costume," was all he said.

"Quid pro quo. Only fair," I said, pointing to his Mozart ensemble.

"I think you look scary, but pretty," Teddy said. "I'd say sexy, too, but I'm your brother, so that's gross."

"How do you even know what *sexy* means?" I asked. "You're six."

"Everyone knows what *sexy* means," he said.

Everyone but me, I guess. But that night, I kind of learned. When we trick-or-treated with Teddy, my own neighbors who'd known me for years didn't recognize me. Guys who'd never given me a second glance did a double take. And every time that happened, I felt a little bit more like the risky sexy chick I was pretending to be. Fake it till you make it actually worked.

The club where Shooting Star was playing was packed. Everyone was in costume, most of the girls in the kinds of racy getups—cleavage-baring French maids, whip-wielding dominatrixes, slutty *Wizard of Oz* Dorothys with skirts hiked up to show their ruby garters—that normally made me feel like a big oaf. I didn't feel oafish at all that night, even if nobody seemed to recognize that I was wearing a costume.

"You were supposed to dress up," a skeleton

guy chastised me before offering me a beer.

"I fucking LOVE those pants," a flapper girl screamed into my ear. "Did you get them in Seattle?"

"Aren't you in the Crack House Quartet?" a guy in a Hillary Clinton mask asked me, referring to some hard-core band that Adam loved and I hated.

When Shooting Star went on, I didn't stay backstage, which is what I normally did. Backstage I could sit on a chair and have an uninterrupted view and not have to talk to anybody. This time, I lingered out by the bar, and then, when the flapper girl grabbed me, I joined her dancing in the mosh pit.

I'd never gone into the mosh pit before. I had little interest in running around in circles while drunk, brawny boys in leather trod on my toes. But tonight, I totally got into it. I understood what it was like to merge your energy with the mob's and to absorb theirs as well. How in the pit, when things got going, you weren't so much walking or dancing as being sucked into a whirlpool.

When Adam finished his set, I was as panting and sweaty as he was. I didn't go backstage to greet him before everyone else got to him. I waited for him to go to the floor of the club, to meet his public like he did at the end of every show. And when he came out, a towel around his neck, sucking on a bottle of water, I flung myself into his arms and kissed him openmouthed and sloppy in front of everyone. I could feel him smiling as he kissed me back.

"Well, well, looks like someone has been infused with spirit of Debbie Harry," he said, wiping some of the lipstick off his chin.

"I guess so. What about you? Are you feeling very Mozarty?"

"All I know about him is from what I saw in that movie. But I remember he was kind of a horndog, so after that kiss, I guess I am. You ready to go? I can load up and we can get out of here."

"No, let's stay for the last set."

"Really?" Adam asked, his eyebrows rising in surprise.

"Yeah. I might even go into the pit with you."

"Have you been drinking?" he teased.

"Just the Kool-Aid," I replied.

We danced, stopping every now and again to make out, until the club closed.

On the way home, Adam held my hand while he drove. Every so often he'd turn to look at me and smile while shaking his head.

"So you like me like this?" I asked.

"Hmm," he responded.

"Is that a yes or a no?"

"Of course I like you."

"No, like this. Did you like me tonight?"

Adam straightened up. "I liked that you got into the show and weren't chomping to leave ASAP. And I loved dancing with you. And I loved how comfortable you seemed to be with all us riffraff."

"But did you like me like this? Like me better?"

"Than what?" he asked. He looked genuinely perplexed.

"Than normal." I was getting irritated now. I'd felt so brazen tonight, like the Halloween costume had imbued me with a new personality, one more worthy of Adam, of my family. I tried to explain that to him, and to my dismay, found myself near tears.

Adam seemed to sense that I was upset. He pulled the car off onto a logging road and turned to me. "Mia, Mia, Mia," he said, stroking the tendrils of my hair that had escaped from the wig. "This *is* the you I like. You definitely dressed sexier and are, you know, blond, and that's different. But the you who you are tonight is the same you I was in love with yesterday, the same you I'll be in love with tomorrow. I love that you're fragile and tough, quiet and kick-ass. Hell, you're one of the punkest girls I know, no matter who you listen to or what you wear."

After that, whenever I started to doubt Adam's feelings, I'd think about my wig, gathering dust in my closet, and it would bring back the memory of that night. And then I wouldn't feel insecure. I'd just feel lucky.

7:13 P.M.

He's here.

I have been hanging out in an empty hospital room in the maternity ward, wanting to be far away from my relatives and even farther away from the ICU and that nurse, or more specifically what that nurse said and what I now understand. I needed to be somewhere where people wouldn't be sad, where the thoughts concerned life, not death. So I came here, the land of screaming babies. Actually, the wail of the newborns is comforting. They have so much fight in them already.

But it's quiet in this room now. So I'm sitting on the windowsill, staring out at the night. A car screeches into the parking garage, shaking me out of my reverie. I peer down in time to catch a glimpse of the taillights of a pink car disappear into the darkness. Sarah, who is the girlfriend of Liz, Shooting Star's drummer, has a pink Dodge Dart. I hold my breath, waiting for Adam to appear out of the tunnel. And then he's here, walking up the ramp, hugging his leather jacket against the winter night. I can see the chain of his wallet glinting in the floodlights. He stops, turns around to talk to someone behind him. I see the soft figure of a woman emerge from the shadows. At first, I think it must be Liz. But then I see the braid.

I wish I could hug her. To thank her for always being one step ahead of what I need.

Of course Kim would go to Adam, to tell him in person as opposed to breaking the news over the phone, and then to bring him here, to me. It was Kim who knew that Adam was playing a show in Portland. Kim who must have somehow managed to cajole her mother into driving downtown. Kim who, judging by Mrs. Schein's absence, must have convinced her mother to go home, to let her stay with Adam and me. I remember how it took Kim two months to get permission to take that helicopter flight with her uncle, so I'm impressed that she managed this amount of emancipation within the space of a few hours. It was Kim who must have braved any number of intimidating bouncers and hipsters to find Adam. And Kim who must have braved telling Adam.

I know this sounds ridiculous, but I'm glad it wasn't me. I don't think I could have borne it. Kim had to bear it.

And now, because of her, he is finally here.

All day long, I've been imagining Adam's arrival, and in my fantasy, I rush to greet him, even though he can't see me and even though, from what I can tell so far, it's nothing like that movie *Ghost*, where you can walk through your loved ones so that they *feel* your presence.

But now that Adam is here, I'm paralyzed. I'm scared to see him. To see his face. I've seen Adam cry twice. Once when we watched *It's a Wonderful Life*. And another time when we were in the train station in Seattle and we saw a mother yelling and swatting her son who had Down syndrome. He just got quiet and it was only when we were walking away that I saw the tears rolling down his cheeks. And it damn near tore my heart out. If he is crying, it *will* kill me. Forget this *my choice* business. That alone will do me in.

I'm such a chickenshit.

I look at the clock on the wall. It's past seven now. Shooting Star will not be opening for Bikini after all. Which is a shame. It was a huge break for them. For a second, I wonder if the rest of the band will go on without Adam. I highly doubt it, though. It's not just that he is the lead singer and the lead guitar player. The band has this kind of code. Loyalty to feelings is important. Last summer, when Liz and Sarah broke up (for what turned out to be all of a month) and Liz was too distraught to play, they canceled their five-night tour, even though this guy Gordon who plays drums in another band offered to sub for her.

I watch Adam make his way to the hospital's main entrance, Kim trailing behind him. Just before he comes to the covered awning and the automatic doors, he looks up into the sky. He is waiting for Kim but I also like to think he's looking for me. His face, illuminated by the lights, is blank, like someone vacuumed away all his personality, leaving only a mask. He doesn't look like him. But at least he's not crying.

That gives me the guts to go to him now. Or rather to me, to the ICU, which is where I know he will want to go. Adam knows Gran and

Gramps and the cousins, and I imagine he'll join the waiting-room vigil later. But right now he's here for me.

Back in the ICU time stands still as always. One of the surgeons who worked on me earlier—the one who sweated a lot and, when it was his turn to pick the music, blasted Weezer—is checking in on me.

The light is dim and artificial and kept to the same level all the time, but even so, the circadian rhythms win out and a nighttime hush has fallen over the place. It is less frenetic than it was during the day, like the nurses and machines are all a little tired and have reverted to power-save mode.

So when Adam's voice reverberates from the hallway outside the ICU, it really wakes everyone up.

"What do you mean I can't go in?" he booms.

I make my way across the ICU, standing just on the other side of the automatic doors. I hear the orderly outside explain to Adam that he is not allowed in this part of the hospital.

"This is bullshit!" Adam yells.

Inside the ward, all the nurses look toward the door, their heavy eyes wary. I am pretty sure they're thinking: *Don't we have enough to deal with inside without having to calm down crazy people outside?*

I want to explain to them that Adam isn't crazy. That he never yells, except for very special occasions.

The graying middle-aged nurse who doesn't attend to the patients but sits by and monitors the computers and phones, gives a little nod and stands up as if accepting a nomination. She straightens her creased white pants and makes her way toward the door. She's really not the best one to talk to him. I wish I could warn them that they ought to send Nurse Ramirez, the one who reassured my grandparents (and freaked me out). She'd be able to calm him down. But this one is only going to make it worse. I follow her through the double doors where Adam and Kim are arguing with an orderly. The orderly looks at the nurse. "I told them they're not authorized to be up here," he explains. The nurse dismisses him with the wave of a hand.

"Can I help you, young man?" she asks Adam. Her voice sounds irritated and impatient, like some of Dad's tenured colleagues at school who Dad says are just counting the days till retirement.

Adam clears his throat, attempting to pull himself together. "I'd like to visit a patient," he says, gesturing toward the doors blocking him from the ICU.

"I'm afraid that's not possible," she replies.

"But my girlfriend, Mia, she's——"

"She's being well cared for," the nurse interrupts. She sounds tired, too tired for sympathy, too tired to be moved by young love.

"I understand that. And I'm grateful for it," Adam says. He's trying his best to play by her rules, to sound mature, but I hear the catch in his voice when he says: "I really need to see her."

"I'm sorry, young man, but visitations are re-stricted to immediate family."

I hear Adam gasp. *Immediate family.* The nurse doesn't mean to be cruel. She's just clueless, but Adam won't know that. I feel the need to protect him and to protect the nurse from what he might do to her. I reach for him, on instinct, even though I cannot really touch him. But his back is to me now. His shoulders are hunched over, his legs start-ing to buckle.

Kim, who was hovering near the wall, is sud-denly at his side, her arms encircling his falling form. With both arms locked around his waist, she turns to the nurse, her eyes blazing with fury. "You don't understand!" she cries.

"Do I need to call security?" the nurse asks.

Adam waves his hand, surrendering to the nurse, to Kim. *"Don't,"* he whispers to Kim.

So Kim doesn't. Without saying another word, she hoists his arm around her shoulder and shifts his weight onto her. Adam has about a foot and fifty pounds on Kim, but after stumbling for a second, she adjusts to the added burden. She bears it.

Kim and I have this theory that almost everything in the world can be divided into two groups.

There are people who like classical music. People who like pop. There are city people. And country people. Coke drinkers. Pepsi drinkers. There are conformists and freethinkers. Virgins and non-virgins. And there are the kind of girls who have boyfriends in high school, and the kind of girls who don't.

Kim and I had always assumed that we both belonged to the latter category. "Not that we'll be forty-year-old virgins or anything," she reassured. "We'll just be the kinds of girls who have boyfriends in college."

That always made sense to me, seemed preferable even. Mom was the sort of girl who had had boyfriends in high school and often remarked that she wished she hadn't wasted her time. "There's only so many times a girl wants to get drunk on Mickey's Big Mouth, go cow-tipping, and make out in back of a pickup truck. As far as the boys I dated were concerned, that amounted to a romantic evening."

Dad, on the other hand, didn't really date till college. He was shy in high school, but then he started playing drums and freshman year of college joined a punk band, and boom, girlfriends. Or at least a few of them until he met Mom, and boom, a wife. I kind of figured it would go that way for me.

So, it was a surprise to both Kim and me when I wound up in Group A, with the boyfriended girls. At first, I tried to hide it. After I came home from the Yo-Yo Ma concert, I told Kim the vaguest of details. I didn't mention the kissing. I rationalized the omission: There was no point getting all worked up about a kiss. One kiss does not a relationship make. I'd kissed boys before, and usually by the next day the kiss had evaporated like a dewdrop in the sun.

Except I knew that with Adam it *was* a big deal. I knew from the way the warmth flooded my whole body that night after he dropped me off at home, kissing me once more at my doorstep. By the way I stayed up until dawn hugging my pillow. By the way that I could not eat the next day, could not wipe the smile off my face. I recognized that the kiss was a door I had walked through. And I knew that I'd left Kim on the other side.

After a week, and a few more stolen kisses, I knew I had to tell Kim. We went for coffee after school. It was May but it was pouring rain as though it were November. I felt slightly suffocated by what I had to do.

"I'll buy. You want one of your froufrou drinks?" I asked. That was another one of the categories we'd determined: people who drank plain coffee and people who drank gussied-up caffeine drinks like the mint-chip lattes Kim was so fond of.

"I think I'll try the cinnamon-spice chai latte," she said, giving me a stern look that said, *I will not be ashamed of my beverage selection.*

I bought us our drinks and a piece of marion-berry pie with two forks. I sat down across from Kim, running the fork along the scalloped edge of the flaky crust.

"I have something to tell you," I said.

"Something about having a boyfriend?" Kim's voice was amused, but even though I was looking down, I could tell that she'd rolled her eyes.

"How'd you know?" I asked, meeting her gaze.

She rolled her eyes again. "Please. Everyone knows. It's the hottest gossip this side of Melanie Farrow dropping out to have a baby. It's like a Democratic presidential candidate marrying a Republican presidential candidate."

"Who said anything about marrying?"

"I'm just being metaphoric," Kim said. "Anyhow, I know. I knew even before you knew."

"Bullshit."

"Come on. A guy like Adam going to a Yo-Yo Ma concert? He was buttering you up."

"It's not like that," I said, though of course, it was totally like that.

"I just don't see why you couldn't tell me sooner," she said in a quiet voice.

I was about to give her my whole one-kiss-not-equaling-a-relationship spiel and to explain that I didn't want to blow it out of proportion, but I stopped myself. "I was afraid you'd be mad at me," I admitted.

"I'm not," Kim said. "But I will be if you ever lie to me again."

"Okay," I said.

"Or if you turn into one of those girlfriends, always ponying around after her boyfriend, and speaking in the first-person plural. '*We* love the winter. *We* think Velvet Underground is seminal.'"

"You know I wouldn't rock-talk to you. First-person singular or plural. I promise."

"Good," Kim replied. "Because if you turn into one of those girls, I'll shoot you."

"If I turn into one of those girls, I'll hand you the gun."

Kim laughed for real at that, and the tension was broken. She popped a hunk of pie into her mouth. "How did your parents take it?"

"Dad went through the five phases of grieving—denial, anger, acceptance, whatever—in like one day. I think he's more freaked out that he is old enough to have a daughter who has a boyfriend." I paused, took a sip of my coffee, letting the word *boyfriend* rest out in the air. "And he claims he can't believe that I'm dating a musician."

"You're a musician," Kim reminded me.

"You know, a punk, pop musician."

"Shooting Star is emo-core," Kim corrected. Unlike me, she cared about the myriad pop musical distinctions: punk, indie, alternative, hard-core, emo-core.

"It's mostly hot air, you know, part of his whole bow-tie-Dad thing. I think Dad likes Adam. He met him when he picked me up for the concert. Now he wants me to bring him over for dinner, but it's only been a week. I'm not quite ready for a meet-the-folks moment yet."

"I don't think I'll ever be ready for that." Kim shuddered at the thought of it. "What about your mom?"

"She offered to take me to Planned Parenthood to get the Pill and told me to make Adam get tested for various diseases. In the meantime, she ordered me to buy condoms now. She even gave me ten bucks to start my supply."

"Have you?" Kim gasped.

"No, it's only been a week," I said. "We're still in the same group on that one."

"For now," Kim said.

One other category that Kim and I devised was people who tried to be cool and people who did not. On this one, I thought that Adam, Kim, and I were in the same column, because even though Adam was cool, he didn't try. It was effortless for him. So, I expected the three of us to become the best of friends. I expected Adam to love everyone I loved as much as I did.

And it did work out like that with my family. He practically became the third kid. But it never clicked with Kim. Adam treated her the way that I'd always imagined he would treat a girl like me. He was nice enough—polite, friendly, but distant. He didn't attempt to enter her world or gain her confidence. I suspected he thought she wasn't cool enough and it made me mad. After we'd been together about three months, we had a huge fight about it.

"I'm not dating Kim. I'm dating you," he said, after I accused him of not being nice enough to her.

"So what? You have lots of female friends. Why not add her to the stable?"

Adam shrugged. "I don't know. It's just not there."

"You're such a snob!" I said, suddenly furious.

Adam eyed me with furrowed brows, like I was a math problem on the blackboard that he was trying to figure out. "How does that make me a snob? You can't force friendship. We just don't have a lot in common."

"*That's* what makes you a snob! You only like people like you," I cried. I stormed out, expecting him to follow after me, begging forgiveness, and when he didn't, my fury doubled. I rode my bike over to Kim's house to vent. She listened to my diatribe, her expression purposefully blasé.

"That's just ridiculous that he only likes people like him," she scolded when I'd finished spewing. "He likes you, and you're not like him."

"That's the problem," I mumbled.

"Well, then deal with that. Don't drag me into your drama," she said. "Besides, I don't really click with him, either."

"You don't?"

"No, Mia. Not everyone swoons for Adam."

"I didn't mean it like that. It's just that I want you guys to be friends."

"Yeah, well, I want to live in New York City and have normal parents. As the man said, 'You can't always get what you want.'"

"But you're two of the most important people in my life."

Kim looked at my red and teary face and her expression softened into a gentle smile. "We know that, Mia. But we're from different parts of your life, just like music and me are from different parts of your life. And that's fine. You don't have to choose one or the other, at least not as far as I'm concerned."

"But I want those parts of my life to come together."

Kim shook her head. "It doesn't work that way. Look, I accept Adam because you love him. And I assume he accepts me because you love me. If it makes you feel any better, your love binds us. And that's enough. Me and him don't have to love each other."

"But I want you to," I wailed.

"Mia," Kim said, an edge of warning in her voice signaling the end of her patience. "You're starting to act like one of those girls. Do you need to get me a gun?"

Later that night, I stopped by Adam's house to say I was sorry. He accepted my apology with a bemused kiss on the nose. And then nothing changed. He and Kim remained cordial but distant, no matter how much I tried to sell them on each other. The funny thing was, I never really bought into Kim's notion that they were somehow bound together through me—until just now when I saw her half carrying him down the hospital corridor.

———

I watch Kim and Adam disappear down the hall. I mean to follow them but I'm glued to the linoleum, unable to move my phantom legs. It's only after they disappear around a corner that I rouse myself and trail after them, but they've already gone inside the elevator.

By now I've figured out that I don't have any supernatural abilities. I can't float through walls or dive down stairwells. I can only do the things I'd be able do in real life, except that apparently what I do in my world is invisible to everyone else. At least that seems to be the case because no one looks twice when I open doors or hit the elevator button. I can touch things, even manipulate door handles and the like, but I can't really *feel* anything or anybody. It's like I'm experiencing everything through a fishbowl. It doesn't really make sense to me, but then again, nothing that's happening today makes much sense.

I assume that Kim and Adam are headed to the waiting room to join the vigil, but when I get there, my family is not there. There's a stack of coats and sweaters on the chairs and I recognize my cousin

Heather's bright orange down jacket. She lives in the country and likes to hike in the woods, so she says that the neon colors are necessary to keep drunk hunters from mistaking her for a bear.

I look at the clock on the wall. It could be dinnertime. I wander back down the halls to the cafeteria, which has the same fried-food, boiled-vegetable stench as cafeterias everywhere. Unappetizing smell aside, it's full of people. The tables are crammed with doctors and nurses and nervous-looking medical students in short white jackets and stethoscopes so shiny that they look like toys. They are all chowing down on cardboard pizza and freeze-dried mashed potatoes. It takes me a while to locate my family, huddled around a table. Gran is chatting to Heather. Gramps is paying careful attention to his turkey sandwich.

Aunt Kate and Aunt Diane are in the corner, whispering about something. "Some cuts and bruises. He was already released from the hospital," Aunt Kate is saying, and for a second I think she's talking about Teddy and am so excited I could cry. But then I hear her say something about there being no alcohol in his system, how our car just swerved into his lane and some guy named Mr. Dunlap says he didn't have time to stop, and then I realize it's not Teddy they're talking about; it's the other driver.

"The police said it was probably the snow, or a deer that caused them to swerve," Aunt Kate continues. "And apparently, this lopsided outcome is fairly common. One party is just fine and the other suffers catastrophic injuries . . ." She trails off.

I don't know that I'd call Mr. Dunlap "just fine," no matter how superficial his injuries. I think about what it must be like to be him, to wake up one Tuesday morning and get into your truck to head off to work at the mill or maybe to the feed-supply store or maybe to Loretta's Diner to have eggs over easy. Mr. Dunlap, who was maybe perfectly happy or perfectly miserable, married with kids or a bachelor. But whatever and whoever he was early this morning, he isn't that person any longer. His life has changed irrevocably, too. If what my aunt says is true, and the crash wasn't his fault, then he was what Kim would call "a poor schmuck," in the wrong place at the wrong time. And because of his bad luck and because he was in his truck, driving eastbound on Route 27 this morning, two kids are now parentless and at least one of them is in grave condition.

How do you live with that? For a second, I have a fantasy of getting better and getting out of here and going to Mr. Dunlap's house, to relieve him of his burden, to reassure him that it's not his fault. Maybe we'd become friends.

Of course, it probably wouldn't work like that. It would be awkward and sad. Besides, I still have no idea what I will decide, still have no clue how I would determine to stay or not stay in the first place. Until I figure that out, I have to leave things up to the fates, or to the doctors, or whoever decides these matters when the decider is too confused to choose between the elevator and the stairs.

I *need* Adam. I take a final look for him and Kim but they're not here, so I head back upstairs to the ICU.

I find them hiding out on the trauma floor, several halls away from the ICU. They're trying to look casual as they test out the doors to various supply closets. When they finally find an unlocked one, they sneak inside. They fumble around in the dark for a light switch. I hate to break it to them, but it's actually back out in the hall.

"I'm not sure this kind of thing works outside of

the movies," Kim tells Adam as she feels along the wall.

"Every fiction has its base in fact," he tells her.

"You don't really look like the doctor type," she says.

"I was hoping for orderly. Or maybe janitor."

"Why would a janitor be in the ICU?" Kim asks. She's a stickler for these kinds of details.

"Broken lightbulb. I don't know. It's all in how you pull it off."

"I still don't understand why you don't just go to her family?" asks Kim, pragmatic as ever. "I'm sure her grandparents could explain, could get you in to see Mia."

Adam shakes his head. "You know, when the nurse threatened to call security, my first thought was 'I'll just call Mia's parents to fix this.'" Adam stops, takes a few breaths. "It just keeps walloping me over and over, and it's like it's the first time every time," he says in a husky voice.

"I know," Kim replies in a whisper.

"Anyhow," Adam says, resuming his search for the light switch, "I can't go to her grandparents. I can't add anything more to their burden. This is something I have to do for myself."

I'm sure my grandparents would actually be

happy to help Adam. They've met him a bunch of times, and they like him a lot. On Christmas, Gran is always sure to make maple fudge for him because he once mentioned how much he liked it.

But I also know that sometimes Adam needs to do things the dramatic way. He is fond of the Grand Gesture. Like saving up two weeks of pizza-delivery tips to take me to Yo-Yo Ma instead of just asking me out on a regular date. Like decorating my windowsill with flowers every day for a week when I was contagious with the chicken pox.

Now I can see that Adam is concentrating on the new task at hand. I'm not sure what exactly he has in mind, but whatever the plan, I'm grateful for it, if only because it's pulled him out of his emotional stupor I saw in the hallway outside the ICU. I've seen him get like this before, when he's writing a new song or is trying to convince me to do something I won't want to do—like go camping with him—and nothing, not a meteorite crashing into the planet, not even a girlfriend in the ICU, can dissuade him.

Besides, it's the girlfriend in the ICU that's necessitating Adam's ruse to begin with. And from what I can guess, it's the oldest hospital trick in the book, taken straight from that movie *The Fugitive*, which

Mom and I recently watched on TNT. I have my doubts about it. So does Kim.

"Don't you think that nurse might recognize you?" Kim asks. "You did yell at her."

"She won't have to recognize me if she doesn't see me. Now I get why you and Mia are such peas in a pod. A pair of Cassandras."

Adam has never met Mrs. Schein, so he doesn't get that implying that Kim is a worrywart is fighting words. Kim scowls, but then I can see her give in. "Maybe this retarded plan of yours would work better if we could actually see what we're doing." She fumbles around in her bag and pulls out the cell phone her mother made her start carrying when she was ten—child LoJack, Kim called it—and turned on the monitor. A square of light softens the darkness.

"Now, that's more like the brilliant girl Mia brags about," Adam says. He turns on his own cell phone and now the room is illuminated by a dull glow.

Unfortunately, the glow shows that the tiny broom closet is full of brooms, a bucket, and a pair of mops, but is lacking any of the disguises that Adam was hoping for. If I could, I would inform them that the hospital has locker rooms, where the doctors and nurses can stow their street clothes and where they change into their scrubs or their lab coats. The only generic hospital garb sitting around are those embarrassing gowns that they put the patients in. Adam probably could throw on a gown and cruise the hallways in a wheelchair with no one the wiser, but such a getup would still not get him into the ICU.

"Shit," Adam says.

"We can keep trying," Kim says, suddenly the cheerleader. "There are like ten floors in this place. I'm sure there are other unlocked closets."

Adam sinks to the floor. "Nah. You're right. This is stupid. We need to come up with a better plan."

"You could fake a drug overdose or something so you wind up in the ICU," Kim says.

"This is Portland. You're lucky if a drug overdose gets you into the ER," Adam replies. "No, I was thinking more like a distraction. You know, like making the fire alarm go off so the nurses all come running out."

"Do you really think sprinklers and panicked nurses are good for Mia?" Kim asks.

"Well, not that exactly, but something so that they all look away for half a second and I stealthily sneak in."

"They'll find you out right away. They'll throw you out on your backside."

"I don't care," Adam responds. "I only need a second."

"Why? I mean what can you do in a second?"

Adam pauses for a second. His eyes, which are normally a kind of mutt's mixture of gray and brown and green, have gone dark. "So I can show her that I'm here. That someone's still here."

Kim doesn't ask any more questions after that. They sit there in silence, each lost in their own thoughts, and it reminds me of how Adam and I can be together but quiet and separate and I realize that they're friends now, friends for real. No matter what happens, at least I have achieved that.

After about five minutes, Adam knocks on his forehead.

"Of course," he says.

"What?"

"Time to activate the Bat Signal."

"Huh?"

"Come on. I'll show you."

When I first started playing the cello, Dad was still playing drums in his band, though that all started to taper off a couple years later when Teddy arrived. But right from the get-go, I could see that there was something different about playing my kind of music, something more than my parents' obvious bewilderment with my classical tastes. My music was solitary. I mean Dad might hammer on his drums for a few hours by himself or write songs alone at the kitchen table, plinking out the notes on his beat-up acoustic guitar, but he always said that songs really got written as you played them. That was what made it so interesting.

When I played, it was most often by myself, in my room. Even when I practiced with the rotating college students, other than during lessons, I still usually played solo. And when I gave a concert or recital, it was alone, on a stage, my cello, myself, and an audience. And unlike Dad's shows, where enthusiastic fans jumped the stage and then dive-bombed into the crowd, there was always a wall between the audience and me. After a while play-ing like this got lonely. It also got kind of boring.

So in the spring of eighth grade I decided to quit. I planned to trail off quietly, by cutting back my obsessive practices, not giving recitals. I figured that if I laid off gradually, by the time I entered high school in the fall, I could start fresh, no longer be known as "the cellist." Maybe then I'd pick up a new instrument, guitar or bass, or even drums.

Plus, with Mom too busy with Teddy to notice the length of my cello practice, and Dad swamped with lesson plans and grading papers at his new teaching job, I figured nobody would even realize that I'd stopped playing until it was already a done deal. At least that's what I told myself. The truth was, I could no sooner quit cello cold turkey than I could stop breathing.

I might have quit for real, were it not for Kim. One afternoon, I invited her to go downtown with me after school.

"It's a weekday. Don't you have practice?" she asked as she twisted the combination on her locker.

"I can skip it today," I said, pretending to search for my earth-science book.

"Have the pod people stolen Mia? First no recitals. And now you're skipping out on practice. What's going on?"

"I don't know," I said, tapping my fingers against the locker. "I'm thinking of trying a new instrument. Like drums. Dad's kit is down in the basement gathering dust."

"Yeah, right. You on drums. That's rich," Kim said with a chuckle.

"I'm serious."

Kim had looked at me, her mouth agape, like I'd

just told her I planned on sautéing up a platter of slugs for dinner. "You can't quit cello," she said after a moment of stunned silence.

"Why not?"

She looked pained as she tried to explain. "I don't know but it just seems like your cello is part of who you are. I can't imagine you without that thing between your legs."

"It's stupid. I can't even play in the school marching band. I mean, who plays the cello anyhow? A bunch of old people. It's a dumb instrument for a girl to play. It's so dorky. And I want to have more free time, to do fun stuff."

"What kind of 'fun stuff'?" Kim challenged.

"Um, you know? Shopping. Hanging out with you . . ."

"Please," Kim said. "You hate to shop. And you hang out with me plenty. But fine, skip practice today. I want to show you something." She took me home with her and dragged out a CD of Nirvana's *MTV Unplugged in New York* and played me "Something in the Way."

"Listen to that," she said. "Two guitar players, a drummer, and a *cello player*. Her name is Lori Goldston and I bet when she was younger, she practiced two hours a day like some other girl I know because if you want to play with the phil-harmonic, or with Nirvana, that's what you have to do. And I don't think anyone would dare call *her* a dork."

I took the CD home and listened to it over and over for the next week, pondering what Kim said. I pulled my cello out a few times, played along. It was a different kind of music than I'd played before, challenging, and strangely invigorating. I planned to play "Something in the Way" for Kim the fol-lowing week when she came over for dinner.

But before I had a chance, at the dinner table Kim casually announced to my parents that she thought I ought to go to summer camp.

"What, you trying to convert me so I'll go to your Torah camp?" I asked.

"Nope. It's music camp." She pulled out a glossy brochure for the Franklin Valley Conservatory, a summer program in British Columbia. "It's for *serious* musicians," Kim said. "You have to send a recording of your playing to get in. I called. The deadline for applications is May first, so there's still time." She turned to face me head-on, as if she were daring me to get mad at her for interfering.

I wasn't mad. My heart was pounding, as if Kim had announced that my family won a lottery and she was about to reveal how much. I looked at her, the nervous look in her eyes betraying the "you wanna piece of me?" smirk on her face, and I was overwhelmed with gratitude to be friends with someone who often seemed to understand me better than I understood myself. Dad asked me if I wanted to go, and when I protested about the money, he said never mind about that. Did I want to go? And I did. More than anything.

Three months later, when Dad dropped me off in a lonely corner of Vancouver Island, I wasn't so sure. The place looked like a typical summer camp, log cabins in the woods, kayaks strewn on the beach. There were about fifty kids who, judging by the way they were hugging and squealing, had all known one another for years. Meanwhile, I didn't know anybody. For the first six hours, no one talked to me except for the camp's assistant director, who assigned me to a cabin, showed me my bunk bed, and pointed the way to the cafeteria, where that night, I was given a plate of something that appeared to be meat loaf.

I stared miserably at my plate, looking out at the gloomy gray evening. I already missed my parents, Kim, and especially Teddy. He was at that fun stage, wanting to try new things and constantly asking "What's that?" and saying the most hilarious things. The day before I left, he informed me that he was "nine-tenths thirsty" and I almost peed myself laughing. Homesick, I sighed and moved the mass of meat loaf around my plate.

"Don't worry, it doesn't rain every day. Just every other day."

I looked up. There was an impish kid who couldn't have been more than ten years old. He had a blond buzz cut and a constellation of freckles falling down his nose.

"I know," I said. "I'm from the Northwest, though it was sunny where I lived this morning. It's the meat loaf I'm worried about."

He laughed. "That doesn't get better. But the peanut-butter-and-jelly is always good," he said, gesturing to a table where a half-dozen kids were fixing themselves sandwiches. "Peter. Trombone. Ontario," he said. This, I would learn, was standard Franklin greeting.

"Oh, hey. I'm Mia. Cello. Oregon, I guess."

Peter told me that he was thirteen, and this was his second summer here; almost everyone started when they were twelve, which is why they all knew one another. Of the fifty students, about half did jazz, the other half classical, so it was a small crew. There were only two other cello players, one of them a tall lanky red-haired guy named Simon who Peter waved over.

"Will you be trying for the concerto competition?" Simon asked me as soon as Peter introduced me as Mia. Cello. Oregon. Simon was Simon. Cello. Leicester, which turned out to be a city in England. It was quite the international group.

"I don't think so. I don't even know what that is," I answered.

"Well, you know how we all perform in an orchestra for the final symphony?" Peter asked me.

I nodded my head, though really I had only a vague idea. Dad had spent the spring reading out loud from the camp's literature, but the only thing I'd cared about was that I was going to camp with other classical musicians. I hadn't paid too much attention to the details.

"It's the summer's end symphony. People from all over come to it. It's a quite a big deal. We, the youngster musicians, play as a sort of cute sideshow," Simon explained. "However, one musician from the camp is chosen to play with the professional orchestra and to perform a solo movement. I came close last year but it went to a flutist. This is my second-to-last chance before I graduate. It hasn't gone to strings in a while, and Tracy, the third of our little trio here, isn't trying out. She's more of a hobby player. Good but not terribly serious. I heard you were serious."

Was I? Not so serious that I hadn't been on the verge of quitting. "How'd you hear that?" I asked.

"The teachers hear all the application reels and word gets around. Your audition tape was apparently quite good. It's unusual to admit someone in year two. So I was hoping for some bloody good competition, to up my game, as it were."

"Whoa, give the girl a chance," Peter said. "She's only just tasted the meat loaf."

Simon shriveled his nose. "Beg pardon. But if you want to put heads together about audition choices, let's have a little chat about that," he said, and disappeared off in the direction of the sundae bar.

"Forgive Simon. We haven't had high-quality cellists for a couple years, so he's excited about new blood. In a purely aesthetic way. He's queer, though it may be hard to tell because he's English."

"Oh. I see. But what did he say? I mean it sounds like he *wants* me to compete against him."

"Of course he does. That's the fun. That's why we're all at camp in the middle of a flipping rain forest," he said, gesturing outside. "That and the amazing cuisine." Peter looked at me. "Isn't that why you're here?"

I shrugged. "I don't know. I haven't played with that many people, at least that many serious people."

Peter scratched his ears. "Really? You said you're from Oregon. Ever done anything with the Portland Cello Project?"

"The what?"

"Avant-garde cello collective, eh. Very interesting work."

"I don't live in Portland," I mumbled, embarrassed that I'd never even *heard* of any Cello Project.

"Well then, who do you play with?"

"Other people. College students mostly."

"No orchestra? No chamber-music ensemble? String quartet?"

I shook my head, remembering a time when one of my student teachers invited me to play in a quartet. I'd turned her down because playing one-on-one with her was one thing; playing with complete strangers was another. I'd always believed that the cello was a solitary instrument, but now I was starting to wonder if maybe *I* was the solitary one.

"Hmm. How are you any good?" Peter asked. "I

don't mean to sound like an asshole, but isn't that how you *get* good? It's like tennis. If you play someone crappy, you end up missing shots or serving all sloppy, but if you play with an ace player, suddenly you're all at the net, hitting good volleys."

"I wouldn't know," I told Peter, feeling like the most boring, sheltered person ever. "I don't play tennis, either."

The next few days went by in a blur. I had no idea why they put out the kayaks. There was no time for playing. Not that kind, anyway. The days were totally grueling. Up at six-thirty, breakfast by seven, private study time for three hours in the morning and in the afternoon, and orchestra rehearsal before dinner.

I'd never played with more than a handful of musicians before, so the first few days in orchestra were chaotic. The camp's musical director, who was also the conductor, scrambled to get us situated and then it was everything he could do to get us playing the most basic of movements in any semblance of time. On the third day, he trotted out some Brahms lullabies. The first time we played, it was painful. The instruments didn't blend so much as collide, like rocks caught in a lawn mower. "Terrible!" he screamed. "How can any of you ever expect to play in a professional orchestra if you cannot keep time on a lullaby? Now again!"

After about a week, it started to gel and I got my first taste of being a cog in the machine. It made me hear the cello in an entirely new way, how its low tones worked in concert with the viola's higher notes, how it provided a foundation for the woodwinds on the other side of the orchestra pit. And even though you might think that being part of a group would make you relax a little, not care so much how you sounded blended among everyone else, if anything, the opposite was true.

I sat behind a seventeen-year-old viola player named Elizabeth. She was one of the most accomplished musicians in the camp—she'd been accepted into the Royal Conservatory of Music in Toronto—and she was also model-gorgeous: tall, regal, with skin the color of coffee, and cheekbones that could carve ice. I would've been tempted to hate her were it not for her playing. If you're not careful, the viola can make the most awful screech, even in the hands of practiced musicians. But with Elizabeth the sound rang out clean and pure and light. Hearing her play, and watching how deeply she lost herself in the music, I wanted to play like that. Better even. It wasn't *just* that I wanted to beat her, but also that I felt like I owed it to her, to the group, to myself, to play at her level.

"That's sounding quite beautiful," Simon said toward the end of camp as he listened to me practice a movement from Haydn's Cello Concerto no. 2, a piece that had given me no end of trouble when I'd first attempted it last spring. "Are you using that for the concerto competition?"

I nodded. Then I couldn't help myself, I grinned. After dinner and before lights-out every night, Simon and I had been bringing our cellos outside to hold impromptu concerts in the long twilight. We took turns challenging each other to cello duels, each trying to out-crazy-play the other. We were *always* competing, always trying to see who could play something better, faster, from memory. It had been so much fun, and was probably one reason why I was feeling so good about the Haydn.

"Ahh, someone's awfully confident. Think you can beat me?" Simon asked.

"At soccer. Definitely," I joked. Simon often told

us that he was the black sheep in his family not because he was gay, or a musician, but because he was such a "shitey footballer."

Simon pretended that I'd shot him in the heart. Then he laughed. "Amazing things happen when you stop hiding behind that hulking beast," he said, gesturing to my cello. I nodded. Simon smiled at me. "Well, don't go getting quite so cocky. You should hear my Mozart. It sounds like the bloody angels singing."

Neither one of us won the solo spot that year. Elizabeth did. And though it would take me four more years, eventually I'd nab the solo.

9:06 P.M.

"I've got exactly twenty minutes before our manager has a total shit fit." Brooke Vega's raspy voice booms in the hospital's now-quiet lobby. So this is Adam's idea: Brooke Vega, the indie-music goddess and lead singer of Bikini. In a trademark punky glam outfit—tonight it's a short bubble skirt, fishnets, high black leather boots, an artfully ripped-up Shooting Star T-shirt, topped off with a vintage fur shrug and a pair of black Jackie O glasses—she stands out in the hospital lobby like an ostrich in a chicken coop. She's surrounded by people: Liz and Sarah; Mike and Fitzy, Shooting Star's rhythm guitarist and bass player, respectively, plus a handful of Portland hipsters who I vaguely recognize. With her magenta hair, she's like the sun, around which her admiring planets revolve. Adam is like a moon, standing off to the side, stroking his chin. Meanwhile, Kim looks shell-shocked, like a bunch of Martians just entered the building. Or maybe it's because Kim worships Brooke Vega. In fact, so does Adam. Aside from me, this was one of the few things they had in common.

"I'll have you out of here in fifteen," Adam promises, stepping into her galaxy.

She strides toward him. "Adam, baby," she croons. "How you holding up?" Brooke encircles him in a hug as if they are old friends, though I know that they only met for the first time today; just yesterday Adam was saying how nervous he was about it. But now she's here acting like his best friend. That's the power of the scene, I guess. As she embraces Adam, I see every guy and girl in that lobby watch hungrily, wishing, I imagine, that their own significant other were upstairs in grave condition so that they might be the ones getting the consolatory cuddle from Brooke.

I can't help but wonder if I were here, if I were watching this as regular old Mia, would I feel jealous, too? Then again, if I were regular old Mia, Brooke Vega would not be in this hospital lobby as part of some great ruse to get Adam in to see me.

"Okay, kids. Time to rock-and-roll. Adam, what's the plan?" Brooke asks.

"*You* are the plan. I hadn't really thought beyond you going up to the ICU and making a ruckus."

Brooke licks her bee-stung lips. "Making a ruckus is one of my favorite things to do. What do you think we should do? Let out a primal scream? Strip? Smash a guitar? Wait, I didn't bring my guitar. Damn."

"You could sing something?" someone suggests.

"How about that old Smiths song 'Girlfriend in a Coma'?" someone calls.

Adam blanches at this sudden reality check and Brooke raises her eyebrows in a stern rebuke. Everyone goes serious.

Kim clears her throat. "Um, it doesn't do us any good if Brooke is a diversion in the lobby. We need to go upstairs to the ICU and then maybe someone could shout that Brooke Vega is here. That might do it. If it doesn't, then sing. All we really want is to lure a couple of curious nurses out, and that grouchy head nurse after them. Once she comes out of the ICU and sees all of us in the hall, she'll be too busy dealing with us to notice that Adam has slipped inside."

Brooke appraises Kim. Kim in her rumpled black pants and unflattering sweater. Then Brooke smiles and links arms with my best friend. "Sounds like a plan. Let's motor, kids."

I lag behind, watching this procession of hipsters barrel through the lobby. The sheer noisiness of them, of their heavy boots, and loud voices, buzzed on by their sense of urgency, ricochets through the quiet hush of the hospital and breathes some life into the place. I remember watching a TV program once about old-age homes that brought in cats and dogs to cheer the elderly and dying patients. Maybe all hospitals should import groups of rabble-rousing punk rockers to kick-start the languishing patients' hearts.

They stop in front of the elevator, waiting endlessly for one empty enough to ferry them up as a group. I decide that I want to be next to my body when Adam makes it to the ICU. I wonder if I will be able to *feel* his touch on me. While they wait at the elevator banks, I scramble up the stairs.

I've been gone from the ICU for more than two hours, and a lot has changed. There is a new patient in one of the empty beds, a middle-aged man whose face looks like one of those surrealist paintings: half of it looks normal, handsome even, the other half is a mess of blood, gauze, and stitching, like someone just blew it off. Maybe a gunshot wound. We get a lot of hunting accidents around here. One of the other patients, one who was so swaddled in gauze and bandages that I couldn't see if he/she was a man or woman, is gone. In his/her place is a woman whose neck is immobilized in one of those collar things.

As for me, I'm off my ventilator now. I remember the social worker telling my grandparents and Aunt Diane that this was a positive step. I stop to check if I feel any different, but I don't feel anything, not physically anyhow. I haven't since I was in the car this morning, listening to Beethoven's Cello Sonata no. 3. Now that I'm breathing on my own, my wall of machines bleeps far less, so I get fewer visits from the nurses. Nurse Ramirez, the one with the nails, looks over at me every now and again, but she's busy with the new guy with the half face.

"Holy crud. Is that Brooke Vega?" I hear some-

one ask in a totally fakey dramatic voice from outside the ICU's automatic doors. I've never heard any
of Adam's friends talk so PG-13 before. It's their
sanitized hospital version of "holy fucking shit."

"You mean Brooke Vega of Bikini? Brooke Vega
who was on the cover of *Spin* magazine last month?
Here in this very hospital?" This time it's Kim talking. She sounds like a six-year-old reciting lines from
a school play about the food groups: *You mean you're
supposed to eat five servings of fruit and vegetables a day?*

"Yeah, that's right," says Brooke's raspy voice.
"I'm here to offer some rock-and-roll succor to all
the people of Portland."

A couple of the younger nurses, the ones who
probably listen to pop radio or watch MTV and
have heard of Bikini, look up, their faces excited
question marks. I hear them whispering, eager to
see if it's really Brooke, or maybe just happy for the
break in the routine.

"Yeah. That's right. So I thought I might
sing a little song. One of my favorites. It's called
'Eraser,'" Brooke says. "One of you guys want to
count me in?"

"I need something to tap with," Liz answers.
"Anyone got some pens or something?"

Now the nurses and orderlies in the ICU are very curious and heading toward the doors. I'm watching it all play out, like a movie on the screen. I stand next to my bed, my eyes trained on the double doors, waiting for them to open. I'm itching with suspense. I think of Adam, of how calming it feels when he touches me, how when he absentmindedly strokes the nape of my neck or blows warm air on my cold hands, I could melt into a puddle.

"What's going on?" the older nurse demands. Suddenly every nurse on the floor is looking at her, not out toward Brooke anymore. No one is going to try to explain to her that a famous pop star is outside. The moment has broken. I feel the tension ease into disappointment. The door isn't going to open.

Outside, I hear Brooke start belting out the lyrics to "Eraser." Even a cappella, even through the automatic double doors, she sounds good.

"Somebody call security *now*," the nurse growls.

"Adam, you better just go for it," Liz yells. "Now or never. Full-court press."

"Go!" screams Kim, suddenly an army general. "We'll cover you."

The door opens. In tumble more than a half-

dozen punkers, Adam, Liz, Fitzy, some people I
don't know, and then Kim. Outside, Brooke is still
singing, as though this were the concert she'd come
to Portland to give.

As Adam and Kim charge through the door,
they both look determined, happy even. I'm
amazed by their resilience, by their hidden pockets of strength. I want to jump up and down
and root for them like I used to do at Teddy's
T-ball games when he'd be rounding third and
heading for home. It's hard to believe, but watching
Kim and Adam in action, I almost feel happy, too.

"Where is she?" Adam yells. "Where's Mia?"

"In the corner, next to the supply closet!" someone shouts. It takes me a minute to realize it's Nurse
Ramirez.

"Security! Get him! Get him!" the grumpy nurse
shouts. She has spotted Adam through all the other
invaders and her face has gone pink with anger.
Two hospital security guards and two orderlies run
inside. "Dude, was that Brooke Vega?" one asks as
he snags Fitzy and flings him toward the exit.

"Think so," the other answers, grabbing Sarah
and steering her out.

Kim has spotted me. "Adam, she's here!" she
screams, and then turns to look at me, the scream

dying in her throat. *"She's here,"* she says again, only this time it's a whimper.

Adam hears her and he is dodging nurses and making his way to me. And then he's there at the foot of my bed, his hand reaching out to touch me. His hand about to be on me. Suddenly I think of our first kiss after the Yo-Yo Ma concert, how I didn't know how badly I'd wanted his lips on mine until the kiss was imminent. I didn't realize just how much I was craving his touch, until now that I can almost feel it on me.

Almost. But suddenly he's moving away from me. Two guards have him by the shoulders and have yanked him back. One of the same guards grabs Kim's elbow and leads her out. She's limp now, offering no resistance.

Brooke's still singing in the hallway. When she sees Adam, she stops. "Sorry, honey," she says. "I gotta jet before I miss my show. Or get arrested." And then she's off down the hall, trailed by a couple of orderlies begging for her autograph.

"Call the police," the old nurse yells. "Have him arrested."

"We're taking him down to security. That's protocol," one guard says.

"Not up to us to arrest," the other adds.

"Just get him off my ward." She harrumphs and turns around. "Miss Ramirez, that had better not have been you abetting these hoodlums."

"Of course not. I was in the supply closet. I missed all the hubbub," she replies. She's such a good liar that her face gives nothing away.

The old nurse claps her hands. "Okay. Show's over. Back to work."

I chase after Adam and Kim, who are being led into the elevators. I jump in with them. Kim looks dazed, like someone flipped her reset button and she's still booting up. Adam's lips are set in a grim line. I can't tell if he's about to cry or about to punch the guard. For his sake, I hope it's the former. For my own, I hope the latter.

Downstairs, the guards hustle Adam and Kim toward a hallway filled with darkened offices. They're about to go inside one of the few offices with lights on when I hear someone scream Adam's name.

"Adam. Stop. Is that you?"

"Willow?" Adam yells.

"Willow?" Kim mumbles.

"Excuse me, where are you taking them?" Willow yells at the guards as she runs toward them.

"I'm sorry but these two were caught trying to break into the ICU," one guard explains.

"Only because they wouldn't let us in," Kim explains weakly.

Willow catches up to them. She's still wearing her nursing clothes, which is strange, because she normally changes out of what she calls "orthopedic couture" as soon as she can. Her long, curly auburn hair looks lank and greasy, like she's forgotten to wash it these past few weeks. And her cheeks, normally rosy like apples, have been repainted beige. "Excuse me. I'm an RN over at Cedar Creek. I did my training here, so if you like we can go straighten this out with Richard Caruthers."

"Who's he?" one guard asks.

"Director of community affairs," the other replies. Then he turns to Willow. "He's not here. It's not business hours."

"Well, I have his home number," Willow says, brandishing her cell phone like a weapon. "I doubt he'd be pleased if I were to call him now and tell him how his hospital was treating someone trying to visit his critically wounded girlfriend. You know that the director values compassion as much as efficiency, and this is not the way to treat a concerned loved one."

"We're just doing our job, ma'am. Following orders."

"How about I save you two the trouble and take it from here. The patient's family is all assembled upstairs. They're waiting for these two to join them. Here, if you have any problems, you tell Mr. Caruthers to get in touch with me." She reaches into her bag and pulls out a card and hands it over. One of the guards looks at it, hands it to the other, who stares at it and shrugs.

"Might as well save ourselves the paperwork," he says. He lets go of Adam, whose body slumps like a scarecrow taken off his pole. "Sorry, kid," he says to Adam, brushing off his shoulders.

"I hope your girlfriend's okay," the other mumbles. And then they disappear toward the glow of some vending machines.

Kim, who has met Willow all of twice, flings herself into her arms. "Thank you!" she murmurs into her neck.

Willow hugs her back, pats her on the shoulders before letting go. She rubs her eyes and winces out a brittle laugh. "What in the hell were you two thinking?" she asks.

"I want to see Mia," Adam says.

Willow turns to look at Adam and it's like someone

has unscrewed her valve, letting all her air escape. She deflates. She reaches out and touches Adam's cheek. "Of course you do." She wipes her eyes with the heel of her hand.

"Are you okay?" Kim asks.

Willow ignores the question. "Let's see about getting you in to Mia."

Adam perks up when he hears this. "You think you can? That old nurse has it in for me."

"If that old nurse is who I think she is, it doesn't matter if she has it in for you. It's not up to her. Let's check in with Mia's grandparents and then I'll find out who's in charge of breaking the rules around here and get you in to see your girl. She needs you now. More than ever."

Adam swivels around and hugs Willow with such force that her feet lift up off the ground.

Willow to the rescue. Just the way she rescued Henry, Dad's best friend and bandmate, who, once upon a time, was a total drunk playboy. When he and Willow had been dating a few weeks, she told him to straighten out and dry out or say good-bye. Dad said that lots of girls had given Henry ultimatums, tried to force him to settle down, and lots of girls had been left crying on the sidewalk. But when Willow packed her toothbrush and told Henry to grow up, Henry was the one who cried. Then he dried his tears, grew up, got sober and monogamous. Eight years later, here they are, with a baby, no less. Willow is formidable that way. Probably why after she and Henry got together she became Mom's best friend; she was another tough-as-nails, tender-as-kittens, feminist bitch. And probably why she was one of Dad's favorite people, even though she hated the Ramones and thought baseball was boring, while Dad lived for the Ramones and thought baseball was a religious institution.

Now Willow is here. Willow the nurse. Willow who doesn't take no for an answer is here. She'll get Adam in to see me. She'll take care of everything. *Hooray!* I want to shout. *Willow is here!*

I'm so busy celebrating Willow's arrival that the implication of her being here takes a few moments to sink in, but when it does, it hits me like a jolt of electricity.

Willow is here. And if she's here, if she's in *my* hospital, it means that there isn't any reason for her to be in *her* hospital. I know her well enough to know that she never would have left him there. Even with me here, she would've stayed with him. He was broken, and brought to her for fixing. He was her patient. Her priority.

I think about the fact that Gran and Gramps are in Portland with me. And that all anyone in that waiting room is talking about is me, how they are avoiding mentioning Mom or Dad or Teddy. I think about Willow's face, which looks like it has been scrubbed clean of all joy. And I think about what she told Adam, that I need him now. More than ever.

And that's how I know. Teddy. He's gone, too.

Mom went into labor three days before Christmas, and she insisted we go holiday shopping together.

"Shouldn't you like lie down or go to the birthing center or something?" I asked.

Mom grimaced through a cramp. "Nah. The contractions aren't that bad and are still like twenty minutes apart. I cleaned our entire house, from top to bottom, while I was in early labor with you."

"Putting the labor in labor," I joked.

"You're a smart-ass, you know that?" Mom said. She took a few breaths. "I've got a ways to go. Now come on. Let's take the bus to the mall. I'm not up to driving."

"Shouldn't we call Dad?" I asked.

Mom laughed at that. "Please, it's enough for me to have to birth *this* baby. I don't need to deal with him, too. We'll call him when I'm ready to pop. I'd much rather have you around."

So Mom and I wandered around the mall, stopping every couple minutes so she could sit down and take deep breaths and squeeze my wrist so hard it left angry red marks. Still, it was a weirdly fun and productive morning. We bought presents for Gran and Gramps (a sweater with an angel on it and a new book about Abraham Lincoln) and toys for the baby and a new pair of rain boots for me. Usually we waited for the holiday sales to buy stuff like that, but Mom said that this year we'd be too busy changing diapers. "Now's not the time to be cheap. Ow, fuck. Sorry, Mia. Come on. Let's go get pie."

We went to Marie Callender's. Mom had a slice of pumpkin and of banana cream. I had blueberry. When she was done, she pushed her plate away and announced she was ready to go to the midwife.

We'd never really talked about my being there or not being there. I went everywhere with Mom and Dad at that point, so it was just kind of assumed. We met a nerve-racked Dad at the birthing center, which was nothing like a doctor's office. It was the ground floor of a house, the inside decked out with beds and Jacuzzi tubs, the medical equipment discreetly tucked away. The hippie midwife led Mom inside and Dad asked me if I wanted to come, too. By now, I could hear Mom screaming profanities.

"I can call Gran and she'll pick you up," Dad said, wincing at Mom's barrage. "This might take a while."

I shook my head. Mom needed me. She'd said so. I sat down on one of the floral couches and picked up a magazine with a goofy-looking bald baby on the cover. Dad disappeared into the room with the bed.

"Music! Goddammit! Music!" Mom screamed.

"We have some lovely Enya. Very soothing," the midwife said.

"Fuck Enya!" Mom screamed. "Melvins. Earth. Now!"

"I've got it covered," Dad said. Then he popped a CD of the loudest, churningest, guitar-heaviest music I'd ever heard. It made all the fast-paced punk songs Dad normally listened to sound like harp music. This music was primal and that seemed to make Mom feel better. She started making these low guttural noises. I just sat there quietly. Every so often she'd scream my name and I'd scamper inside. Mom would look up at me, her face plastered with sweat. *Don't be scared,* she'd whisper. *Women can handle the worst kind of pain. You'll find out one day.* Then she'd scream *fuck* again.

I'd seen a couple of births on that cable-TV show, and people usually yelled for a while; sometimes they swore and it had to be bleeped, but it never took longer than half an hour. After three hours, Mom and the Melvins were still screaming along. The whole birthing center felt tropically humid, even though it was forty degrees outside.

Henry dropped by. When he came inside and heard the noise, he froze in his tracks. I knew that the whole kid-thing freaked him out. I'd overheard Mom and Dad talking about that, and Henry's refusal to grow up. He'd apparently been shocked when Mom and Dad had me, and now was completely bewildered that they chose to have a second. They'd both been relieved when he and Willow had gotten back together. "Finally, a grown-up in Henry's life," Mom had said.

Henry looked at me; his face was pale and sweaty. "Holy shit, Mee. Should you be hearing this? Should *I* be hearing this?"

I shrugged. Henry sat down next to me. "I've got the flu or something, but your dad just called asking me to bring some food. So here I am," he said, proffering a Taco Bell bag reeking of onions. Mom let out another moan. "I should go. Don't want me spreading germs or anything." Mom screamed even louder and Henry practically jumped in his seat. "You sure you wanna hang around for this? You can come back to my place. Willow's there, taking care of me." He grinned when he mentioned her name. "She can take care of you, too." He stood up to leave.

"No. I'm fine. Mom needs me. Dad's kind of freaking out, though."

"Did he puke yet?" Henry asked, sitting back down on the couch. I laughed, but then saw from his face that he was serious.

"He threw up when you were coming. Almost fainted on the floor. Not that I can blame him. But the dude was a mess, the doctors wanted to kick him out . . . said they were going to if you didn't come out within a half hour. That got your mom so pissed off she pushed you out five minutes later." Henry smiled, leaning back into the sofa. "So the story goes. But I'll tell you this: He cried like a motherfucking baby when you were born."

"I've heard that part."

"Heard what part?" Dad asked breathlessly. He grabbed the bag from Henry. "Taco Bell, Henry?"

"Dinner of champions," Henry said.

"It'll do. I'm starving. It's intense in there. Got to keep up my strength."

Henry winked at me. Dad pulled out a burrito and offered one to me. I shook my head. Dad had started unwrapping his meal when Mom let out a growl and then started screaming at the midwife that she was ready to push.

The midwife poked her head out the door. "I think we're getting close, so maybe you should save dinner for later," she said. "Come on back."

Henry practically bolted out the front door. I followed Dad into the bedroom where Mom was sitting now, panting like a sick dog. "Would you like to watch?" the midwife asked Dad, but he just swayed and turned a pale shade of green.

"I'm probably better up here," he said, grasping Mom's hand, which she violently shook off.

No one asked me if I wanted to watch. I just automatically went to stand next to the midwife. It was pretty gross, I'll admit. Lots of blood. And I'd certainly never seen my mom so full-on frontal before. But it felt strangely normal for me to be there. The midwife was telling Mom to push, then hold, then push. "Go baby, go baby, go baby go," she chanted. "You're almost there!" she cheered. Mom looked like she wanted to smack her.

When Teddy slid out, he was head up, facing the ceiling, so that the first thing he saw was me. He didn't come out squalling like you see on TV. He was just quiet. His eyes were open, staring straight at me. He held my gaze as the midwife suctioned out his nose. "It's a boy," she shouted.

The midwife put Teddy on Mom's belly. "Do you want to cut the cord?" she asked Dad. Dad waved his hands no, too overcome or nauseous to speak.

"I'll do it," I offered.

The midwife held the cord taut and told me where to cut. Teddy lay still, his gray eyes wide open, still staring at me.

Mom always said that it was because Teddy saw me first, and because I cut his cord, that somewhere deep down he thought I was his mother. "It's like those goslings," Mom joked. "Imprinting on a zoologist, not the mama goose, because he was the first one they saw when they hatched."

She exaggerated. Teddy didn't really think I was his mother, but there were certain things that only I could do for him. When he was a baby and going through his nightly fussy period, he'd only calm down after I played him a lullaby on my cello. When he started getting into Harry Potter, only I was allowed to read a chapter to him every night. And when he'd skin a knee or bump his head, if I was around he would not stop crying until I bestowed a magic kiss on the injury, after which he'd miraculously recover.

I know that all the magic kisses in the world probably couldn't have helped him today. But I would do anything to have been able to give him one.

10:40 P.M.

I run away.

I leave Adam, Kim, and Willow in the lobby and I just start careening through the hospital. I don't realize I'm looking for the pediatric ward until I get there. I tear through the halls, past rooms with nervous four-year-olds sleeping restlessly before tomorrow's tonsillectomies, past the neonatal ICU with babies the size of fists, hooked up to more tubes than I am, past the pediatric oncology unit where bald cancer patients sleep under cheerful murals of rainbows and balloons. I'm looking for him, even though I know I won't find him. Still, I have to keep looking.

I picture his head, his tight blond curls. I love to nuzzle my face in those curls, have done since he was a baby. I kept waiting for the day when he'd swat me away, say "You're embarrassing me," the way he does to Dad when Dad cheers too loudly at T-ball games. But so far, that hadn't happened. So far, I've been allowed constant access to that head of his. So far. Now there is no more so far. It's over.

I picture myself nuzzling his head one last time, and I can't even imagine it without seeing myself crying, my tears turning his blond curlicues straight.

Teddy is never going to graduate from T-ball to baseball. He's never going to grow a mustache. Never going to get into a fistfight or shoot a deer or kiss a girl or have sex or fall in love or get married or father his own curly-haired child. I'm only ten years older than him, but it's like I've already had so much more life. It is unfair. If one of us should have been left behind, if one of us should be given the opportunity for more life, it should be him.

I race through the hospital like a trapped wild animal. *Teddy?* I call. *Where are you? Come back to me!*

But he won't. I know it's fruitless. I give up and drag myself back to my ICU. I want to break the double doors. I want to smash the nurses' station. I want it all to go away. *I* want to go away. I don't want to be here. I don't want to be in this hospital. I don't want to be in this suspended state where I can see what's happening, where I'm aware of what I'm feeling without being able to actually feel it. I cannot scream until my throat hurts or break a window with my fist until my hand bleeds, or pull my hair out in clumps until the pain in my scalp overcomes the one in my heart.

I'm staring at myself, at the "live" Mia now, lying in her hospital bed. I feel a burst of fury. If I could slap my own lifeless face, I would.

Instead, I sit down in the chair and close my eyes, wishing it all away. Except I can't. I can't concentrate because there's suddenly so much noise. My monitors are blipping and chirping and two nurses are racing toward me.

"Her BP and pulse ox are dropping," one yells.

"She's tachycardic," the other yells. "What happened?"

"Code blue, code blue in Trauma," blares the PA.

Soon the nurses are joined by a bleary-eyed doctor, rubbing the sleep out of his eyes, which are ringed by deep circles. He yanks down the covers and lifts my hospital gown. I'm naked from the waist down, but no one notices these things here. He puts his hands on my belly, which is swollen and hard. His eyes widen and then narrow into slits. "Abdomen's rigid," he says angrily. "We need to do an ultrasound."

Nurse Ramirez runs to a back room and then wheels out what looks like a portable laptop with a long white attachment. She squirts some jelly on my stomach, and the doctor runs the attachment over my stomach.

"Damn. Full of fluid," he says. "Patient had surgery this afternoon?"

"A splenectomy," Nurse Ramirez replies.

"Could be a missed blood vessel that wasn't cauterized," the doctor says. "Or a slow leak from a perforated bowel. Car accident, right?"

"Yes. Patient was medevaced in this morning."

The doctor flips through my chart. "Doctor

Sorensen was her surgeon. He's still on call. Page him, get her to the OR. We need to get inside and find out what's leaking, and why, before she drops any further. Jesus, brain contusions, collapsed lung. This kid's a train wreck."

Nurse Ramirez shoots the doctor a dirty look, as if he had just insulted me.

"Miss Ramirez," the grumpy nurse at the desk scolds. "You have patients of your own to deal with. Let's get this young woman intubated and transferred to the OR. That will do her more good than all this dillydallying around!"

The nurses work rapidly to detach the monitors and catheters and run another tube down my throat. A pair of orderlies rush in with a gurney and heave me onto it. I'm still naked from the waist down as they hustle me out, but right before I reach the back door, Nurse Ramirez calls, "Wait!" and then gently closes the hospital gown around my legs. She taps me three times on the forehead with her fingers, like it's some kind of Morse code message. And then I'm gone into the maze of hallways leading toward the OR for another round of cutting, but this time I don't follow myself. This time I stay behind in the ICU.

I am starting to get it now. I mean, I don't totally

fully understand. It's not like I somehow commanded a blood vessel to pop open and start leaking into my stomach. It's not like I wished for another surgery. But Teddy is gone. Mom and Dad are gone. This morning I went for a drive with my family. And now I am here, as alone as I've ever been. I am seventeen years old. This is not how it's supposed to be. This is not how my life is supposed to turn out.

In the quiet corner of the ICU I start to really think about the bitter things I've managed to ignore so far today. What would it be like if I stay? What would it feel like to wake up an orphan? To never smell Dad smoke a pipe? To never stand next to Mom quietly talking as we do the dishes? To never read Teddy another chapter of *Harry Potter*? To stay without them?

I'm not sure this is a world I belong in anymore. I'm not sure that I want to wake up.

I've only ever been to one funeral in my life and it was for someone I hardly knew.

I might have gone to Great-Aunt Glo's funeral after she died of acute pancreatitis. Except her will was very specific about her final wishes. No traditional service, no burial in the family plot. Instead, she wanted to be cremated and have her ashes scattered in a sacred Native American ceremony somewhere in the Sierra Nevada Mountains. Gran was pretty annoyed by that, by Aunt Glo in general, who Gran said was always trying to call attention to how different she was, even after she was dead. Gran ended up boycotting the ash scattering, and if she wasn't going, there was no reason for the rest of us to.

Peter Hellman, my trombonist friend from conservatory camp, he died two years ago, but I didn't find out until I returned to camp and he wasn't there. Few of us had known that he'd had lymphoma. That was the funny thing about conservatory camp; you got so close with the people over the summer, but it was some unwritten rule that you didn't keep in touch during the rest of the year. We were summer friends. Anyhow, we had a memorial concert at camp in Peter's honor, but it wasn't really a funeral.

Kerry Gifford was a musician in town, one of Mom and Dad's people. Unlike Dad and Henry, who as they got older and had families became less music performers than music connoisseurs, Kerry stayed single and stayed faithful to his first love: playing music. He was in three bands and he earned his living doing the sound at a local club, an ideal setup because at least one of his bands seemed to play there every week, so he just had to hop up on the stage and let someone take the controls for his set, though sometimes you'd see him jumping down in the middle of a set to adjust the monitors himself. I had known Kerry when I was little and would go to shows with Mom and Dad and then I sort of remet him when Adam and I got together and I started going to shows again.

He was at work one night, doing the sound for a Portland band called Clod, when he just keeled over on the soundboard. He was dead by the time the ambulance got there. A freak brain aneurysm.

Kerry's death caused an uproar in our town. He was kind of a fixture around here, an outspoken guy with a big personality and this mass of wild white-boy dreadlocks. And he was young, only thirty-two. Everyone we knew was planning on going to his funeral, which was being held in the town where he grew up, in the mountains a couple of hours' drive away. Mom and Dad were going, of course, and so was Adam. So even though I felt a little bit like an impostor crashing someone's death day, I decided to go along. Teddy stayed with Gran and Gramps.

We caravanned to Kerry's hometown with a bunch of people, squeezing into a car with Henry and Willow, who was so pregnant the seat belt wouldn't fit over her bump. Everyone took turns telling funny stories about Kerry. Kerry the avowed left-winger who decided to protest the Iraq war by getting a bunch of guys to dress up in drag and go down to the local army recruiting office to enlist. Kerry the atheist curmudgeon, who hated how commercialized Christmas had become and so threw an annual Merry Anti-Christmas Celebration at the club, where he held a contest for which band could play the most distorted versions of Christmas carols. Then he invited everyone to throw all their crappy presents into a big pile in the middle of the club. And contrary to local lore, Kerry did not burn the stuff in a bonfire; Dad told me that he donated it to St. Vincent de Paul.

As everyone talked about Kerry, the mood in the car was fizzy and fun, like we were going to the circus, not a funeral. But it seemed right, it seemed true to Kerry, who was always overflowing with frenetic energy.

The funeral, though, was the opposite. It was

horribly depressing—and not just because it was for someone who'd died tragically young and for no particular reason aside from some bad arterial luck. It was held in a huge church, which seemed strange considering Kerry was an outspoken atheist, but that part I could understand. I mean where else do you have a funeral? The problem was the service itself. It was obvious that the pastor had never even met Kerry because when he talked about him, it was generic, about what a kind heart Kerry had and how even though it was sad that he was gone, he was getting his "heavenly reward."

And instead of having eulogies from his bandmates or the people in town who he'd spent the last fifteen years with, some uncle from Boise got up and talked about teaching Kerry how to ride a bike when he was six, like learning to ride a bike was the defining moment in Kerry's life. He concluded by reassuring us that Kerry was walking with Jesus now. I could see my mom getting red when he said that, and I started to get a little worried that she might say something. We went to church sometimes, so it's not like Mom had anything against religion, but Kerry totally did and Mom was ferociously protective of the people she loved, so much that she took insults upon them personally.

Her friends sometimes called her Mama Bear for this reason. Steam was practically blowing out of Mom's ears by the time the service ended with a rousing rendition of Bette Midler's "Wind Beneath My Wings."

"It's a good thing Kerry's dead, because that funeral would've sent him over the edge," Henry said. After the church service, we'd decided to skip the formal luncheon and had gone to a diner.

"'Wind Beneath My Wings'?" Adam asked, absentmindedly taking my hand into his and blowing on it, which is what he did to warm my perpetually cold fingers. "What's wrong with 'Amazing Grace'? It's still traditional—"

"But doesn't make you want to puke," Henry interjected. "Or better yet, 'Three Little Birds' by Bob Marley. That would have been a more Kerry-worthy song. Something to toast the guy he was."

"That funeral wasn't about celebrating Kerry's life," Mom growled, yanking at her scarf. "It was about repudiating it. It was like they killed him all over again."

Dad put a calming hand over Mom's clenched fist. "Now come on. It was just a song."

"It wasn't just a song," Mom said, snatching her hand away. "It was what it represented. That whole

charade back there. You of all people should understand."

Dad shrugged and smiled sadly. "Maybe I should.
But I can't be angry with his family. I imagine this
funeral was their way of reclaiming their son."

"Please," Mom said, shaking her head. "If they
wanted to claim their son, why didn't they respect
the life he chose to live? How come they never
came to visit? Or supported his music?"

"We don't know what they thought about all
that," Dad replied. "Let's not judge too harshly. It
has to be heartbreaking to bury your child."

"I can't believe you're making excuses for them,"
Mom exclaimed.

"I'm not. I just think you might be reading too
much into a musical selection."

"And I think you're confusing being empathetic
with being a pushover!"

Dad's wince was barely visible, but it was enough
to make Adam squeeze my hand and Henry and
Willow exchange a look. Henry jumped in, to Dad's
rescue, I think. "It's different for you, with your parents," he told Dad. "I mean they're old-fashioned
but they always were into what you did, and even
in your wildest days, you were always a good son, a
good father. Always home for Sunday dinner."

Mom guffawed, as if Henry's statement had proven her point. We all turned to her, and our shocked expressions seemed to snap her out of her rant. "Clearly I'm just emotional right now," she said. Dad seemed to understand that was as much an apology as he was going to get right now. He covered her hand with his and this time she didn't snatch it away.

Dad paused, hesitating before speaking. "I just think that funerals are a lot like death itself. You can have your wishes, your plans, but at the end of the day, it's out of your control."

"No way," Henry said. "Not if you make your wishes known to the right people." He turned to Willow and spoke to the bump in her belly. "So listen up, family. At my funeral no one is allowed to wear black. And for music, I want something poppy and old-school, like Mr. T Experience." He looked up at Willow. "Got that?"

"Mr. T Experience. I'll make sure of it."

"Thanks, and what about you, honey?" he asked her.

Without missing a beat, Willow said: "Play 'P.S. You Rock My World' by the Eels. And I want one of those green funerals where they bury you in the ground under a tree. So the funeral itself would be in nature. And no flowers. I mean, give me all the peonies you want when I'm alive, but once I'm dead, better to give donations on my behalf to a good charity like Doctors Without Borders."

"You've got all the details figured out," Adam said. "Is that a nurse thing?"

Willow shrugged.

"According to Kim, that means you're deep," I said. "She says that the world is divided into the people who imagine their own funerals and the people who don't, and that smart and artistic people naturally fall into the former category."

"So which are you?" Adam asked me.

"I'd want Mozart's Requiem," I said. I turned to Mom and Dad. "Don't worry, I'm not suicidal or anything."

"Please," Mom said, her mood lightening as she stirred her coffee. "When I was growing up I'd have elaborate fantasies about my funeral. My dead-beat father and all the friends who'd wronged me would weep over my casket, which would be red, naturally, and they'd play James Taylor."

"Let me guess," Willow said. "'Fire and Rain'?"

Mom nodded and she and Willow started laughing and soon everyone at the table was cracking up so hard that tears ran down our faces. And then we were crying, even me, who didn't know Kerry all that well. Crying and laughing, laughing and crying.

"So what now?" Adam asked Mom when we'd calmed down. "Still harbor a soft spot for Mr. Taylor?"

Mom stopped and blinked hard, which is what she does when she's thinking about something. Then she reached over to stroke Dad's cheek, a rare demonstration of PDA. "In my ideal scenario, my bighearted pushover husband and I die quickly and simultaneously when we're ninety-two years old. I'm not sure how. Maybe we're on a safari in Africa—'cause in the future, we're rich; hey, it's my fantasy—and we come down with some exotic sickness and go to sleep one night feeling fine and then never wake up. And no James Taylor. Mia plays at our funeral. If, that is, we can tear her away from the New York Philharmonic."

Dad was wrong. It's true you might not get to control your funeral, but sometimes you *do* get to choose your death. And I can't help thinking that part of Mom's wish *did* come true. She went with Dad. But I won't be playing at her funeral. It's possible that her funeral will also be mine. There's something comforting in that. To go down as a family. No one left behind. That said, I can't help thinking Mom would *not* be happy about this. In fact, Mama Bear would be absolutely furious with the way events are unfolding today.

2:48 A.M.

I'm back where I started. Back in the ICU. My body, that is. *I've* been sitting here all along, too tired to move. I wish I could go to sleep. I wish there was some kind of anesthesia for *me*, or at least something to make the world shut up. I want to be like my body, quiet and lifeless, putty in someone else's hands. I don't have the energy for this decision. I don't want this anymore. I say it out loud. *I don't want this*. I look around the ICU, feeling kind of ridiculous. I doubt all the other messed-up people in the ward are exactly thrilled to be here, either.

My body wasn't gone from the ICU for too long. A few hours for surgery. Some time in the recovery room. I don't know exactly what's happened to me, and for the first time today, I don't really care. I shouldn't have to care. I shouldn't have to work this hard. I realize now that dying is easy. Living is hard.

I'm back on the ventilator, and once again there's tape over my eyes. I still don't understand the tape. Are the doctors afraid that I'll wake up mid-surgery and be horrified by the scalpels or blood? As if those things could faze me now. Two nurses, the one assigned to me and Nurse Ramirez, come over to my bed and check all my monitors. They call out a chorus of numbers that are as familiar to me now as my own name: BP, pulse ox, respiratory rate. Nurse Ramirez looks like an entirely different person from the one who arrived here yesterday afternoon. The makeup has all rubbed off and her hair is flat. She looks like she could sleep standing up. Her shift must be over soon. I'll miss her but I'm glad she'll be able to get away from me, from this place. I'd like to get away, too. I think I will. I think it's just a matter of time—of figuring out how to let go.

I haven't been back in my bed fifteen minutes when Willow shows up. She marches through the double doors and goes to speak to the one nurse behind the desk. I don't hear what she says, but I hear her tone: it's polite, soft-spoken, but leaving no room for questions. When she leaves the room a few minutes later, there's a change in the air. Willow's in charge now. The grumpy nurse at first looks pissed off, like *Who is this woman to tell me what to do?* But then she seems to resign, to throw her hands up in surrender. It's been a crazy night. The shift is almost over. Why bother? Soon, me and all of my noisy, pushy visitors will be somebody else's problem.

Five minutes later, Willow is back, bringing Gran and Gramps with her. Willow has worked all day and now she is here all night. I know she doesn't get enough sleep on a good day. I used to hear Mom give her tips for getting the baby to sleep through the night.

I'm not sure who looks worse, me or Gramps. His cheeks are sallow, his skin looks gray and papery, and his eyes are bloodshot. Gran, on the other hand, looks just like Gran. No sign of wear and tear on her. It's like exhaustion wouldn't dare mess with her. She bustles right over to my bed.

"You've sure got us on a roller-coaster ride today," Gran says lightly. "Your mom always said she couldn't believe what an easy girl you were and I remember telling her, 'Just wait until she hits puberty.' But you proved me wrong. Even then you were such a breeze. Never gave us any trouble. Never the kind of girl to make my heart race in fear. You made up for a lifetime of that today."

"Now, now," Gramps says, putting a hand on her shoulder.

"Oh, I'm only kidding. Mia would appreciate it. She's got a sense of humor, no matter how serious she sometimes seems. A wicked sense of humor, this one."

Gran pulls the chair up next to my bed and starts combing through my hair with her fingers. Someone has rinsed it out, so, while it's not exactly clean, it's not caked with blood, either. Gran starts untangling my bangs, which are about chin length. I'm forever cutting bangs, then growing them. It's about as radical a makeover as I can give myself. She works her way down, pulling the hair out from under the pillow so it streams down my chest, hiding some of the lines and tubes connected to me. "There, much better," she says. "You know, I went outside for a walk today and you'll never guess what I saw. A crossbill. In Portland in February. Now, that's unusual. I think it's Glo. She always had a soft spot for you. Said you reminded her of your father, and she adored him. When he cut his first crazy Mohawk hairdo, she practically threw him a party.

She loved that he was rebellious, so different. Little did she know your father couldn't stand her. She came to visit us once when your dad was around five or six, and she had this ratty mink coat with her. This was before she got all into the animal rights and crystals and the like. The coat smelled terrible, like mothballs, like the old linens we kept in a trunk in the attic, and your father took to calling her 'Auntie Trunk Smell.' She never knew that. But she loved that he'd rebelled against us, or so she thought, and she thought it was something that you rebelled all over again by becoming a classical musician. Though much as I tried to tell her that it wasn't the way it was, she didn't care. She had her own ideas about things; I suppose we all do."

Gran twitters on for another five minutes, filling me in on mundane news: Heather has decided she wants to become a librarian. My cousin Matthew bought a motorcycle and my aunt Patricia is not pleased about that. I've heard her keep up a running stream of commentary like this for hours while she's cooking dinner or potting orchids. And listening to her now, I can almost picture us in her greenhouse, where even in winter, the air is always warm and humid and smells musty and earthy like soil with the slightest tinge of manure. Gran hand-collects cowshit, "cow patties," she calls them, and mixes them in with mulch to make her own fertilizer. Gramps thinks she should patent the recipe and sell it because she uses it on her orchids, which are always winning awards.

I try to meditate on the sound of Gran's voice, to be carried away by her happy babble. Sometimes I can almost fall asleep while sitting on the bar stool at her kitchen counter and listening to her, and I wonder if I could do that here today. Sleep would be so welcome. A warm blanket of black to erase everything else. Sleep without dreams. I've heard people talk about the sleep of the dead. Is that what death would feel like? The nicest, warmest, heaviest never-ending nap? If that's what it's like, I wouldn't mind. If that's what dying is like, I wouldn't mind that at all.

I jerk myself up, a panic destroying whatever calm listening to Gran had offered. I am still not entirely clear on the particulars here, but I do know that once I fully commit to going, I'll go. But I'm not ready. Not yet. I don't know why, but I'm not. And I'm a little scared that if I accidentally think, *I wouldn't mind an endless nap*, it will happen and be irreversible, like the way my grandparents used to warn me that if I made a funny face as the clock struck noon, it would remain like that forever.

I wonder if every dying person gets to decide whether they stay or go. It seems unlikely. After all, this hospital is full of people having poisonous chemicals pumped into their veins or submitting to horrible operations all so they can stay, but some of them will die anyway.

Did Mom and Dad decide? It hardly seems like there would have been time for them to make such a momentous decision, and I can't imagine them choosing to leave me behind. And what about Teddy? Did he want to go with Mom and Dad? Did he know that I was still here? Even if he did, I wouldn't blame him for choosing to go without me. He's little. He was probably scared. I suddenly picture him alone and frightened, and for the first time in my life, I hope that Gran is right about the angels. I pray they were all too busy comforting Teddy to worry about me.

Why can't someone else decide this for me? Why can't I get a death proxy? Or do what baseball teams do when it's late in the game and they need a solid batter to bring the guys on base home? Can't I have a pinch hitter to take me home?

Gran is gone. Willow is gone. The ICU is tranquil. I close my eyes. When I open them again,

Gramps is there. He's crying. He's not making any noise, but tears are cascading down his cheeks, wetting his entire face. I've never seen anyone cry like this. Quiet but gushing, a faucet behind his eyes mysteriously turned on. The tears fall onto my blanket, onto my freshly combed hair. *Plink. Plink. Plink.*

Gramps doesn't wipe his face or blow his nose. He just lets the tears fall where they may. And when the well of grief is momentarily dry, he steps forward and kisses me on the forehead. He looks like he's about to leave, but then he doubles back to my bedside, bends so his face is level with my ear, and whispers into it.

"It's okay," he tells me. "If you want to go. Everyone wants you to stay. *I* want you to stay more than I've ever wanted anything in my life." His voice cracks with emotion. He stops, clears his throat, takes a breath, and continues. "But that's what I want and I could see why it might not be what you want. So I just wanted to tell you that I understand if you go. It's okay if you have to leave us. It's okay if you want to stop fighting."

For the first time since I realized that Teddy was gone, too, I feel something unclench. I feel myself breathe. I know that Gramps can't be that late-inning pinch hitter I'd hoped for. He won't unplug my breathing tube or overdose me with morphine or anything like that. But this is the first time today that anyone has acknowledged what I have lost. I know that the social worker warned Gran and Gramps not to upset me, but Gramps's recognition, and the permission he just offered me—it feels like a gift.

Gramps doesn't leave me. He slumps back into the chair. It's quiet now. So quiet that you can almost hear other people's dreams. So quiet that you can almost hear me tell Gramps, "Thank you."

When Mom had Teddy, Dad was still playing drums in the same band he'd been in since college. They'd released a couple of CDs; they'd gone on a tour every summer. The band was by no means big, but they had a following in the Northwest and in various college towns between here and Chicago. And, weirdly, they had a bunch of fans in Japan. The band was always getting letters from Japanese teenagers begging them to come play, and offering up their homes as crash pads. Dad was always saying that if they went, he'd take me and Mom. Mom and I even learned a few words of

Japanese just in case. *Konnichiwa. Arigatou.* It never panned out, though.

After Mom announced she was pregnant with Teddy, the first sign that changes were afoot was when Dad went and got himself a learner's permit. At age thirty-three. He tried letting Mom teach him to drive, but she was too impatient, he said. Dad was too sensitive to criticism, Mom said. So Gramps took Dad out along the empty country lanes in his pickup truck, just like he'd done with the rest of Dad's siblings—except they'd all learned to drive when they were sixteen.

Next up was the wardrobe change, but it wasn't something any of us noticed right away. It wasn't like one day he stripped off the tight black jeans and band tees in exchange for suits. It was more subtle. First the band tees went out in the window in favor of button-up 1950s rayon numbers, which he dug up at the Goodwill until they started getting trendy and he had to buy them from the fancy vintage-clothing shop. Then the jeans went in the bin, except for one pair of impeccable, dark blue Levi's, which Dad ironed and wore on weekends. Most days he wore neat, flat-front cuffed trousers. But when, a few weeks after Teddy was born, Dad gave away his leather jacket—his prized beat-up motorcycle jacket with the fuzzy leopard belt—we finally realized that a major transformation was under way.

"Dude, you cannot be serious," Henry said when Dad handed him the jacket. "You've been wearing this thing since you were a kid. It even smells like you."

Dad shrugged, ending the conversation. Then he went to pick up Teddy, who was squalling from his bassinet.

A few months later, Dad announced he was leaving the band. Mom told him not to do it for her sake. She said it was okay to keep playing as long as he didn't take off on monthlong tours, leaving her alone with two kids. Dad said not to worry, he wasn't quitting for her.

Dad's other bandmates took his decision in stride, but Henry was devastated. He tried to talk him out of it. Promised they'd only play in town. Wouldn't have to tour. Ever be gone overnight. "We can even start playing shows in suits. We'll look like the Rat Pack. Do Sinatra covers. Come on, man," Henry reasoned.

When Dad refused to reconsider, he and Henry had a huge blowout. Henry was furious with Dad for unilaterally quitting the band, especially since Mom had said he could still play shows. Dad told Henry that he was sorry, but he'd made his decision. By this time, he'd already filled out his applications for grad school. He was going to be a teacher now. No more dicking around. "One day you'll understand," Dad told Henry.

"The fuck I will," Henry shot back.

Henry didn't speak to Dad for a few months after that. Willow would drop by from time to time, to play peacemaker. She'd explain to Dad that Henry was just sorting some stuff out. "Give him time," she said, and Dad would pretend to not be hurt. Then she and Mom would drink coffee in the kitchen and exchange knowing smiles that seemed to say: *Men are such boys.*

Henry eventually resurfaced, but he didn't apologize to Dad, not right away, anyhow. Years later, shortly after his daughter was born, Henry called our house one night in tears. "I get it now," he told Dad.

Strangely enough, in some ways Gramps seemed as upset with Dad's metamorphosis as Henry had been. You would have thought he would love the new Dad. On the surface, he and Gran seem so old-school, it's like a time warp. They don't use computers or watch cable TV, and they never curse and have this thing about them that makes you want to be polite. Mom, who swore like a prison guard, never cursed around Gran and Gramps. It was like no one wanted to disappoint them.

Gran got a kick out of Dad's stylistic transformation. "Had I known that all that stuff was going to come back in style, I would've saved Gramps's old suits," Gran said one Sunday afternoon when we'd stopped by for lunch and Dad pulled off a trench coat to reveal a pair of wool gabardine trousers and a 1950s cardigan.

"It hasn't come back into style. *Punk* has come into style, so I think this is your son's way of rebelling all over again," Mom said with a smirk. "Whose daddy's a rebel? Is your daddy a rebel?" Mom baby-talked as Teddy gurgled in delight.

"Well, he sure does look dapper," Gran said. "Don't you think?" she said, turning to Gramps.

Gramps shrugged. "He always looks good to me. All my children and grandchildren do." But he looked pained as he said it.

Later that afternoon, I went outside with Gramps to help him collect firewood. He needed to split some more logs, so I watched him take an ax to a bunch of dried alder.

"Gramps, don't you like Dad's new clothes?" I asked.

Gramps halted the ax in midair. Then he set it down gently next to the bench I was sitting on. "I like his clothes just fine, Mia," he said.

"But you looked so sad in there when Gran was talking about it."

Gramps shook his head. "Don't miss a thing, do you? Even at ten years old."

"It's not easy to miss. When you feel sad, you *look* sad."

"I'm not sad. Your father seems happy and I think he'll make a good teacher. Those are some lucky kids who get to read *The Great Gatsby* with your dad. I'll just miss the music."

"Music? You never go to Dad's shows."

"I've got bad ears. From the war. The noise hurts."

"You should wear headphones. Mom makes me do that. Earplugs just fall out."

"Maybe I'll try that. But I've always listened to your dad's music. At low volume. I'll admit, I don't much care for all that electric guitar. Not my cup of tea. But I still admired the music. The words, especially. When he was about your age, your father used to come up with these great stories. He'd sit down at his little table and write them down, then give them to Gran to type up, then he'd draw pictures. Funny stories about animals, but real and smart. Always reminded me of that book about the spider and the pig—what's it called?"

"*Charlotte's Web*?"

"That's the one. I always thought your dad would grow up to be a writer. And in a way, I always felt like he did. The words he writes to his music, they're poetry. You ever listen carefully to the things he says?"

I shook my head, suddenly ashamed. I hadn't even realized that Dad wrote lyrics. He didn't sing so I just assumed that the people in front of the microphones wrote the words. But I *had* seen him sit at the kitchen table with a guitar and a notepad a hundred times. I'd just never put it together.

That night when we got home, I went up to my room with Dad's CDs and a Discman. I checked the liner notes to see which songs Dad had written and then I painstakingly copied down all the lyrics. It was only after I saw them scrawled in my science lab book that I saw what Gramps meant. Dad's lyrics were not just rhymes. They were something else. There was one song in particular called "Waiting for Vengeance" that I listened to and read over and over until I had it memorized. It was on the second album, and it was the only slow song they ever did; it sounded almost country, probably from Henry's brief infatuation with hillbilly punk. I listened to it so much that I started singing it to myself without even realizing it.

> *Well, what is this?*
> *What am I coming to?*
> *And beyond that, what am I gonna do?*
> *Now there's blankness*
> *Where once your eyes held the light*
> *But that was so long ago*
> *That was last night*

> *Well, what was that?*
> *What's that sound that I hear?*
> *It's just my lifetime*
> *It's whistling past my ear*
> *And when I look back*

Everything seems smaller than life
The way it's been for so long
Since last night

Now I'm leaving
Any moment I'll be gone
I think you'll notice
I think you'll wonder what went wrong
I'm not choosing
But I'm running out of fight
And this was decided so long ago
It was last night

"What are you singing, Mia?" Dad asked me, catching me serenading Teddy as I pushed him around the kitchen in his stroller in a vain attempt to get him to nap.

"Your song," I said sheepishly, suddenly feeling like I'd maybe illegally trespassed into Dad's private territory. Was it wrong to go around singing other people's music without their permission?

But Dad looked delighted. "My Mia's singing 'Waiting for Vengeance' to my Teddy. What do you think about that?" He leaned over to muss my hair and to tickle Teddy on his chubby cheek. "Well, don't let me stop you. Keep going. I'll take over this part," he said, taking the stroller.

I felt embarrassed to sing in front of him now, so I just sort of mumbled along, but then Dad joined in and we sang softly together until Teddy fell asleep. Then he put a finger over his lips and gestured for me to follow him into the living room.

"Want to play some chess?" he asked. He was always trying to teach me to play, but I thought it was too much work for a supposed game.

"How about checkers?" I asked.

"Sure."

We played in silence. When it was Dad's move, I'd steal looks at him in his button-down shirt, trying to remember the fast-fading picture of the guy with peroxided hair and a leather jacket.

"Dad?"

"Hmm."

"Can I ask you a question?"

"Always."

"Are you sad that you aren't in a band anymore?"

"Nope," he said.

"Not even a little bit?"

Dad's gray eyes met mine. "What brought this all on?"

"I was talking to Gramps."

"Oh, I see."

"You do?"

Dad nodded. "Gramps thinks that he somehow exerted pressure on me to change my life."

"Well, did he?"

"I suppose in an indirect way he did. By being who he is, by showing me what a father is."

"But you were a good dad when you played in a band. The *best* dad. I wouldn't want you to give that up for me," I said, feeling suddenly choked up. "And I don't think Teddy would, either."

Dad smiled and patted my hand. "Mia Oh-My-Uh. I'm not giving anything up. It's not an either-or proposition. Teaching or music. Jeans or suits. Music will always be a part of my life."

"But you quit the band! Gave up dressing punk!"

Dad sighed. "It wasn't hard to do. I'd played that part of my life out. It was time. I didn't even think twice about it, in spite of what Gramps or Henry might think. Sometimes you make choices in life and sometimes choices make you. Does that make any sense?"

I thought about the cello. How sometimes I didn't understand why I'd been drawn to it, how some days it seemed as if the instrument had chosen me. I nodded, smiled, and returned my attention to the game. "King me," I said.

4:57 A.M.

I can't stop thinking about "Waiting for Vengeance." It's been years since I've listened to or thought of that song, but after Gramps left my bedside, I've been singing it to myself over and over. Dad wrote the song ages ago, but now it feels like he wrote it yesterday. Like he wrote it from wherever he is. Like there's a secret message in it for me. How else to explain those lyrics? *I'm not choosing. But I'm running out of fight.*

What does it mean? Is it supposed to be some kind of instruction? Some clue about what my parents would choose for me if they could? I try to think about it from their perspectives. I know they'd want to be with me, for us all to be together again eventually. But I have no idea if that even happens after you die, and if it does, it'll happen whether I go this morning or in seventy years. What would they want for me *now*? As soon as I pose the question, I can see Mom's pissed-off expression. She'd be livid with me for even contemplating anything *but* staying. But Dad, he understood what it meant to run out of fight. Maybe, like Gramps, he'd understand why I don't think I *can* stay.

I'm singing the song, as if buried within its lyrics are instructions, a musical road map to where I'm supposed to go and how to get there.

I'm singing and concentrating and singing and thinking so hard that I barely register Willow's return to the ICU, barely notice that she's talking to the grumpy nurse, barely recognize the steely determination in her tone.

Had I been paying attention, I might have realized that Willow was lobbying for Adam to be able to visit me. Had I been paying attention, I might have somehow got away before Willow was—as always—successful.

I don't want to see him now. I mean, of course I do. I ache to. But I know that if I see him, I'm going to lose the last wisp of peacefulness that Gramps gave me when he told me that it was okay to go. I'm trying to summon the courage to do what I have to do. And Adam will complicate things. I try to stand up to get away, but something has happened to me since I went back into surgery. I no longer have the strength to move. It takes all my effort to sit upright in my chair. I can't run away; all I can do is hide. I curl my knees into my chest and close my eyes.

I hear Nurse Ramirez talking to Willow. "I'll take him over," she says. And for once, the grumpy nurse doesn't order her back to her own patients.

"That was a pretty boneheaded move you pulled earlier," I hear her tell Adam.

"I know," Adam answers. His voice is a throaty whisper, the way it gets after a particularly screamy concert. "I was desperate."

"No, you were romantic," she tells him.

"I was idiotic. They said she was doing better before. That she'd come off the ventilator. That she was getting stronger. But after I came in here that she got worse. They said her heart stopped on the operating table . . ." Adam trails off.

"And they got it started. She had a perforated bowel that was slowly leaking bile into her abdomen and it threw her organs out of whack. This kind of thing happens all the time, and it had nothing to do with you. We caught it and fixed it and that's what matters."

"But she was doing better," Adam whispers. He sounds so young and vulnerable, like Teddy used to sound when he got the stomach flu. "And then I came in and she almost died." His voice chokes into a sob. The sound of it wakes me up like a bucket of ice water dropped down my shirt. Adam thinks that *he* did this to me? No! That's beyond absurd. He's so wrong.

"And I *almost* stayed in Puerto Rico to marry a fat SOB," the nurse snaps. "But I di'int. And I have a different life now. *Almost* don't matter. You got to deal with the situation at hand. And she's still here." She whips the privacy curtain around my bed. "In you go," she tells Adam.

I force my head up and my eyes open. Adam. God, even in this state, he is beautiful. His eyes are dipping with fatigue. He's sprouting stubble, enough of it that if we were to make out, it would make my chin raw. He is wearing his typical band uniform of a T-shirt, skinny pegged pants, and Converse, with Gramps's plaid scarf draped over his shoulders.

When he first sees me, he blanches, like I'm some hideous Creature from the Black Lagoon. I do look pretty bad, hooked back up to the ventilator and a dozen other tubes, the dressing from my latest surgery seeping blood. But after a moment, Adam exhales loudly and then he's just Adam again. He searches around, like he's dropped something and then finds what he's looking for: my hand.

"Jesus, Mia, your hands are freezing." He squats down, takes my right hand into his, and careful to not bump into my tubes and wires, draws his mouth to them, blowing warm air into the shelter he's created. "You and your crazy hands." Adam is always amazed at how even in the middle of summer, even after the sweatiest of encounters, my hands stay cold. I tell him it's bad circulation but he doesn't buy it because my feet are usually warm. He says I have bionic hands, that this is why I'm such a good cello player.

I watch him warm my hands as he has done a thousand times before. I think of the first time he did it, at school, sitting on the lawn, as if it were the most natural thing in the world. I also remember the first time he did it in front of my parents. We were all sitting on the porch on Christmas Eve, drinking cider. It was freezing outside. Adam grabbed my hands and blew on them. Teddy giggled. Mom and Dad didn't say anything, just exchanged a quick look, something private that passed between them and then Mom smiled ruefully at us.

I wonder if I tried, if I could feel him touching me. If I were to lie down on top of myself in the bed, would I become one with my body again?

Would I feel him then? If I reached out my ghostly hand to his, would he feel me? Would he warm the hands he cannot see?

Adam drops my hand and steps forward to look at me. He is standing so close that I can almost smell him and I'm overpowered by the need to touch him. It's basic, primal, and all-consuming the way a baby needs its mother's breast. Even though I know, if we touch, a new tug-of-war—one that will be even more painful than the quiet one Adam and I have been waging these past few months— will begin.

Adam is mumbling something now. In a low voice. Over and over he is saying: please. *Please. Please. Please. Please. Please. Please. Please. Please. Please.* Finally, he stops and looks at my face. "Please, Mia," he implores. "Don't make me write a song."

I'd never expected to fall in love. I was never the kind of girl who had crushes on rock stars or fantasies about marrying Brad Pitt. I sort of vaguely knew that one day I'd probably have boyfriends (in college, if Kim's prediction was anything to go by) and get married. I wasn't totally immune to the charms of the opposite sex, but I wasn't one of those romantic, swoony girls who had pink fluffy daydreams about falling in love.

Even as I was falling in love—full throttle, intense, can't-erase-that-goofy-smile love—I didn't really register what was happening. When I was with Adam, at least after those first few awkward weeks, I felt so good that I didn't bother thinking about what was going on with me, with us. It just felt normal and right, like slipping into a hot bubble bath. Which isn't to say we didn't fight. We argued over lots of stuff: him not being nice enough to Kim, me being antisocial at shows, how fast he drove, how I stole the covers. I got upset because he never wrote any songs about me. He claimed he wasn't good with sappy love songs: "If you want a song, you'll have to cheat on me or something," he said, knowing full well that wasn't going to happen.

This past fall, though, Adam and I started to have a different kind of fight. It wasn't even a fight, really. We didn't shout. We barely even argued, but a snake of tension quietly slithered into our lives. And it seemed like it all started with my Juilliard audition.

"So did you knock them dead?" Adam asked me

when I got back. "They gonna let you in with a full scholarship?"

I had a feeling that they were going to let me in, at least—even before I told Professor Christie about the one judge's "long time since we've had an Oregon country girl" comment, even before she hyperventilated because she was so convinced this was a tacit promise of admission. Something had happened to my playing in that audition; I had broken through some invisible barrier and could finally play the pieces like I heard them being played in my head, and the result had been something transcendent: the mental and physical, the technical and emotional sides of my abilities all finally blending. Then, on the drive home, as Gramps and I were approaching the California-Oregon border, I just had this sudden flash—a vision of me lugging a cello through New York City. And it was like I *knew*, and that certainty planted itself in my belly like a warm secret. I'm not the kind of person who's prone to premonitions or overconfidence, so I suspected that there was more to my flash than magical thinking.

"I did okay," I told Adam, and as I said it, I realized that I'd just straight-out lied to him for the first time, and that this was different from all the lying by omission I'd been doing before.

I had neglected to tell Adam that I was applying to Juilliard in the first place, which was actually harder than it sounded. Before I sent in my application, I had to practice every spare moment with Professor Christie to fine-tune the Shostakovich concerto and the two Bach suites. When Adam asked me why I was so busy, I gave purposely vague excuses about learning tough new pieces. I justified this to myself because it was technically true. And then Professor Christie arranged for me to have a recording session at the university so I could submit a high-quality CD to Juilliard. I had to be at the studio at seven in the morning on a Sunday and the night before I'd pretended to be feeling out of sorts and told Adam he probably shouldn't stay over. I'd justified that fib, too. I *was* feeling out of sorts because I was so nervous. So, it wasn't a real lie. And besides, I thought, there was no point in making a big fuss about it. I hadn't told Kim, either, so it wasn't like Adam was getting special deception treatment.

But after I told him I'd only done okay at the audition, I had the feeling that I was wading into quicksand, and that if I took one more step, there'd be no extricating myself and I'd sink until I suffocated. So I took a deep breath and heaved myself back onto solid ground. "Actually, that's not true," I told Adam. "I did really well. I played better than I ever have in my life. It was like I was possessed."

Adam's first reaction was to smile with pride. "I wish I could've seen that." But then his eyes clouded over and his lips fell into a frown. "Why'd you downplay it?" he asked. "Why didn't you call me after the audition to brag?"

"I don't know," I said.

"Well, this is great news," Adam said, trying to mask his hurt. "We should be celebrating."

"Okay, let's celebrate," I said, with a forced gaiety. "We can go to Portland Saturday. Go to the Japanese Gardens and go out for dinner at Beau Thai."

Adam grimaced. "I can't. We're playing in Olympia and Seattle this weekend. Minitour. Re-member? I'd love for you to come, but I don't know if that's really a celebration for you. But I'll be back Sunday late afternoon. I can meet you in Portland Sunday night if you want."

"I can't. I'm playing in a string quartet at some professor's house. What about next weekend?"

Adam looked pained. "We're in the studio the next couple weekends, but we can go out during the week somewhere. Around here. To the Mexi-can place?"

"Sure. The Mexican place," I said.

Two minutes before, I hadn't even wanted to celebrate, but now I was feeling dejected and insulted at being relegated to a midweek dinner at the same place we always went to.

When Adam graduated from high school last spring and moved out of his parents' place and into the House of Rock, I hadn't expected much to change. He'd still live nearby. We'd still see each other all the time. I'd miss our little powwows in the music wing, but I would also be relieved to have our relationship out from under the microscope of high school.

But things had changed when Adam moved into the House of Rock and started college, though not for the reasons I'd thought they would. At the beginning of the fall, just as Adam was getting used to college life, things suddenly started heating up with Shooting Star. The band was offered a record deal with a medium-size label based in Seattle and now were busy in the studio recording. They were also playing more shows, to larger and larger crowds, almost every weekend. Things were so hectic that Adam had dropped half his course load and was going to college part-time, and if things kept up at this rate, he was thinking of dropping out altogether. "There are no second chances," he told me.

I was genuinely excited for him. I knew that Shooting Star was something special, more than just a college-town band. I hadn't minded Adam's increasing absences, especially since he made it so clear how much *he* minded them. But somehow, the prospect of Juilliard made things different— somehow it made me mind. Which didn't make any sense at all because if anything, it should have leveled the field. Now I had something exciting happening, too.

"We can go to Portland in a few weeks," Adam promised. "When all the holiday lights are up."

"Okay," I said sullenly.

Adam sighed. "Things are getting complicated, aren't they?"

"Yeah. Our schedules are too busy," I said.

"That's not what I meant," Adam said, turning my face toward his so I was looking at him in the eye.

"I know that's not what you meant," I replied, but then a lump lodged itself in my throat and I couldn't talk anymore.

We tried to defuse the tension, to talk about it without really talking about it, to joke-ify it.

"You know I read in *US News and World Report* that Willamette University has a good music program," Adam told me. "It's in Salem, which is apparently getting hipper by the moment."

"According to who? The governor?" I replied.

"Liz found some good stuff at a vintage-clothing store there. And you know, once the vintage places come in, the hipsters aren't far behind."

"You forget, I'm not a hipster," I reminded him. "But speaking of, maybe Shooting Star should move to New York. I mean, it's the heart of the punk scene. The Ramones. Blondie." My tone was frothy and flirtatious, an Oscar-worthy performance.

"That was thirty years ago," Adam said. "And even if I wanted to move to New York, there's no way the rest of the band would." He stared mournfully at his shoes and I recognized the joking part of the conversation had ended. My stomach lurched, an appetizer before the full portion of heartache I had a feeling was going to be served at some point soon.

Adam and I had never been the kind of couple to talk about the future, about where our relationship was going, but with things suddenly so unclear, we avoided talking about *anything* that was happening more than a few weeks away, and this made our conversations as stilted and awkward as they'd been in those early weeks together before we'd found our groove. One afternoon in the fall, I spotted a beautiful 1930s silk gown in the vintage store where Dad bought his suits and I almost pointed it out to Adam and asked if he thought I should wear that to the prom, but prom was in June and maybe Adam would be on tour in June or maybe I'd be too busy getting ready for Juilliard, so I didn't say anything. Not long after that, Adam was complaining about his decrepit guitar, saying he wanted to get a vintage Gibson SG, and I offered to get it for him for his birthday. But then he said that those guitars cost thousands of dollars, and besides his birthday wasn't until September, and the way he said *September*, it was like a judge issuing a prison sentence.

A few weeks ago, we went to a New Year's Eve party together. Adam got drunk, and when midnight came, he kissed me hard. "Promise me. Promise me you'll spend New Year's with me next year," he whispered into my ear.

I was about to explain that even if I did go to Juilliard, I'd be home for Christmas and New Year's, but then I realized that wasn't the point. So

I promised him because I wanted it to be true as much as he did. And I kissed him back so hard, like I was trying to merge our bodies through our lips.

On New Year's Day, I came home to find the rest of my family gathered in the kitchen with Henry, Willow, and the baby. Dad was making breakfast: smoked-salmon hash, his specialty.

Henry shook his head when he saw me. "Look at the kids today. Seems like just yesterday that stumbling home at eight o'clock felt early. Now I'd kill just to be able to sleep until eight."

"We didn't even make it till midnight," Willow admitted, bouncing the baby on her lap. "Good thing, because this little lady decided to start her new year at five-thirty."

"I stayed up till midnight!" Teddy yelled. "I saw the ball drop on TV at twelve. It's in New York, you know? If you move there, will you take me to see it drop in real life?" he asked

"Sure, Teddy," I said, feigning enthusiasm. The idea of me going to New York was seeming more and more real, and though this generally filled me with a nervous, if conflicted, excitement, the image of me and Teddy hanging out together on New Year's Eve left me feeling unbearably lonely.

Mom looked at me, eyebrows arched. "It's New

Year's Day, so I won't give you shit for coming in at this hour. But if you're hungover, you're grounded."

"I'm not. I had one beer. I'm just tired."

"Just tired, is it? You sure?" Mom grabbed ahold of my wrist and turned me toward her. When she saw my stricken expression, she tilted her head to the side as if to say, *You okay?* I shrugged and bit my lip to keep from losing it. Mom nodded. She handed me a cup of coffee and led me to the table. She put down a plate of hash and a thick slice of sourdough bread, and even though I couldn't imagine being hungry, my mouth watered and my stomach rumbled and I was suddenly ravenous. I ate silently, Mom watching me all the while. After everyone was done, Mom sent the rest of them into the living room to watch the Rose Parade on TV.

"Everyone out," she ordered. "Mia and I will do the washing up."

As soon as everyone was gone, Mom turned to me and I just fell against her, crying and releasing all of the tension and uncertainty of the last few weeks. She stood there silently, letting me blubber all over her sweater. When I stopped, she held out the sponge. "You wash. I'll dry. We'll talk. I always find it calming. The warm water, the soap."

Mom picked up the dish towel and we went to

work. And I told her about Adam and me. "It was like we had this perfect year and a half," I said. "So perfect that I never even thought about the future. About it taking us in different directions."

Mom's smile was both sad and knowing. "*I* thought about it."

I turned to her. She was staring straight out the window, watching a couple of sparrows bathe in a puddle. "I remember last year when Adam came over for Christmas Eve. I told your father that you'd fallen in love too soon."

"I know, I know. What does a dumb kid know about love?"

Mom stopped drying a skillet. "That's not what I meant. The opposite, really. You and Adam never struck me as a 'high-school' relationship," Mom said, making quote marks with her hands. "It was nothing like the drunken roll in the back of some guy's Chevy that passed for a relationship when I was in high school. You guys seemed, still seem, in love, truly, deeply." She sighed. "But seventeen is an inconvenient time to be in love."

That made me smile and made the pit in my stomach soften a little. "Tell me about it," I said. "Though if we weren't both musicians, we could go to college together and be fine."

"That's a cop-out, Mia," Mom countered. "All relationships are tough. Just like with music, sometimes you have harmony and other times you have cacophony. I don't have to tell you that."

"I guess you're right."

"And come on, music brought you two together. That's what your father and I always thought. You were both in love with music and then you fell in love with each other. It was a little like that for your dad and me. I didn't play but I listened. Luckily, I was a little older when we met."

I'd never told Mom about what Adam had said that night after the Yo-Yo Ma concert, when I'd asked him *Why me?* How the music was totally a part of it. "Yeah, but now I feel like it's music that's going to pull us apart."

Mom shook her head. "That's bullshit. Music can't do that. Life might take you down different roads. But each of you gets to decide which one to take." She turned to face me. "Adam's not trying to stop you going to Juilliard, is he?"

"No more than I'm trying to get him to move to New York. And it's all ridiculous anyway. I might not even go."

"No, you might not. But you're going somewhere. I think we all get that. And the same is true for Adam."

"At least he can go somewhere while still living here."

Mom shrugged. "Maybe. For now anyhow."

I put my face in my hands and shook my head. "What am I going to do?" I lamented. "I feel like I'm caught in a tug-of-war."

Mom shot me a sympathetic grimace. "I don't know. But I do know that if you want to stay and be with him, I'd support that, though maybe I'm only saying that because I don't think you'd be able to turn down Juilliard. But I'd understand if you chose love, Adam love, over music love. Either way you win. And either way you lose. What can I tell you? Love's a bitch."

Adam and I talked about it once more after that. We were at House of Rock, sitting on his futon. He was riffing about on his acoustic guitar.

"I might not get in," I told him. "I might wind up at school here, with you. In a way, I hope I don't get accepted so I don't have to choose."

"If you get in, the choice is already made, isn't it?" Adam asked.

It was. I would go. It didn't mean I'd stop loving

Adam or that we'd break up, but Mom and Adam were both right. I wouldn't turn down Juilliard.

Adam was silent for a minute, plinking away at his guitar so loud that I almost missed it when he said, "I don't want to be the guy who doesn't want you to go. If the tables were turned, you'd let me go."

"I kind of already have. In a way, you're already gone. To your own Juilliard," I said.

"I know," Adam said quietly. "But I'm still here. And I'm still crazy in love with you."

"Me, too," I said. And then we stopped talking for a while as Adam strummed an unfamiliar melody. I asked him what he was playing.

"I'm calling it 'The Girlfriend's-Going-to-Juilliard-Leaving-My-Punk-Heart-in-Shreds Blues,'" he said, singing the title in an exaggeratedly twangy voice. Then he smiled that goofy shy smile that I felt like came from the truest part of him. "I'm kidding."

"Good," I said.

"Sort of," he added.

5:42 A.M.

Adam is gone. He suddenly rushed out, calling to Nurse Ramirez that he'd forgotten something important and would be back as soon as he could. He was already out the door when she told him that she was about to get off work. In fact, she just left, but not before making sure to inform the nurse who'd relieved Old Grumpy that "the young man with the skinny pants and messy hair" is allowed to see me when he returns.

Not that it matters. Willow rules the school now. She has been marching the troops through here all morning. After Gran and Gramps and Adam, Aunt Kate stopped by. Then it was Aunt Diane and Uncle Greg. Then my cousins shuffled in. Willow's running to and fro, a gleam in her eye. She's up to something, but whether it's trotting out loved ones to lobby on behalf of my continuing my earthly existence or whether she's simply bringing them in to say good-bye, I can't say.

Now it's Kim's turn. Poor Kim. She looks like she slept in a Dumpster. Her hair has staged a full-scale rebellion and more of it has escaped her mangled braid than remains tucked inside. She's wearing one of what she calls her "turd sweaters," the greenish, grayish, brownish lumpy masses her mom is always buying her. At first, Kim squints at me, as if I'm a bright, glaring light. But then it's like she adjusts to the light and decides that even though I may look like a zombie, even though there are tubes sticking out of every which orifice, even though there's blood on my thin blanket from where it's seeped through the bandages, I'm still Mia and she's still Kim. And what do Mia and Kim like to do more than anything? Talk.

Kim settles into the chair next to my bed. "How are you doing?" she asks.

I'm not sure. I'm exhausted, but at the same time Adam's visit has left me . . . I don't know what. Agitated. Anxious. Awake, definitely awake. Though I couldn't feel it when he touched me, his presence stirred me up anyhow. I was just starting to feel grateful that he was here when he booked out of here like the devil was chasing him. Adam has spent the last ten hours trying to get in to see me, and now that he finally succeeded, he left ten minutes after arriving. Maybe I scared him. Maybe he doesn't want to deal. Maybe I'm not the only chickenshit around here. After all, I spent the last day dreaming of him coming to me, and when he finally staggered into the ICU, if I had the strength, I would've run away.

"Well, you would not believe the crazy night it's been," Kim says. Then she starts telling me about it. About her mom's hysterics, about how she lost it in front of my relatives, who were very gracious about the whole thing. The fight they had outside the Roseland Theater in front of a bunch of punks and hipsters. When Kim shouted at her crying mother to "pull it together and start acting like the adult around here" and then stalked off into the club leaving a shocked Mrs. Schein at the curb, a group of guys in spiked leather and fluorescent hair cheered and high-fived her. She tells me about Adam, his determination to get in to see me, how after he got kicked out of the ICU, he enlisted the help of his music friends, who were not at all the snobby scenesters she'd imagined them to be. Then she told me that a bona fide rock star had come to the hospital on my behalf.

Of course, I know almost everything that Kim is telling me, but there is no way that she'd know that. Besides, I like having her recount the day to me. I like how Kim is talking to me normally, like Gran did earlier, just jabbering on, spinning a good yarn, as if we were together on my porch, drinking coffee (or an iced caramel frappuccino in Kim's case) and catching up.

I don't know if once you die you remember

things that happened to you when you were alive. It makes a certain logical sense that you wouldn't. That being dead will feel like before you were born, which is to say, a whole lot of nothingness. Except that for me, at least, my prebirth years aren't entirely blank. Every now and again, Mom or Dad will be telling a story about something, about Dad catching his first salmon with Gramps, or Mom remembering the amazing Dead Moon concert she saw with Dad on their first date, and I'll have an overpowering déjà vu. Not just a sense that I've heard the story before, but that I've lived it. I can picture myself sitting on the riverbank as Dad pulls a hot-pink coho out of the water, even though Dad was all of twelve at the time. Or I can hear the feedback when Dead Moon played "D.O.A." at the X-Ray, even though I've never heard Dead Moon play live, even though the X-Ray Café shut down before I was born. But sometimes the memories feel so real, so visceral, so personal, that I confuse them with my own.

I never told anyone about these "memories." Mom probably would've said that I was there—as one of the eggs in her ovaries. Dad would've joked that he and Mom had tortured me with their stories one too many times and had inadvertently brainwashed me. And Gran would've told me that maybe I *was* there as an angel before I chose to become Mom and Dad's kid.

But now I wonder. And now I hope. Because when I go, I want to remember Kim. And I want to remember her like this: telling a funny story, fighting with her crazy mom, being cheered on by punkers, rising to the occasion, finding little pockets of strength in herself that she had no idea she possessed.

Adam is a different story. Remembering Adam would be like losing him all over again, and I'm not sure if I can bear that on top of everything else.

Kim's up to the part of Operation Distraction, when Brooke Vega and a dozen assorted punks descended upon the hospital. She tells me that before they got to the ICU, she was so scared of getting into trouble, but how when she burst inside the ward, she'd felt exhilarated. When the guard had grabbed her, she hadn't been scared at all. "I kept thinking, what's the worst that could happen? I go to jail. Mom has a conniption. I get grounded for a year." She stops for a minute. "But after what's happened today, that would be nothing. Even going to jail would be easy compared to losing you."

I know that Kim's telling me this to try to keep

me alive. She probably doesn't realize that in a weird way, her remark frees me, just like Gramps's permission did. I know it will be awful for Kim when I die, but I also think about what she said, about not being scared, about jail being easy compared to losing me. And that's how I know that Kim will be okay. Losing me will hurt; it will be the kind of pain that won't feel real at first, and when it does, it will take her breath away. And the rest of her senior year will probably suck, what with her getting all that cloying your-best-friend's-dead sympathy that will drive her so crazy, and also because really, we are each other's only close friend at school. But she'll deal. She'll move on. She'll leave Oregon. She'll go to college. She'll make new friends. She'll fall in love. She'll become a photographer, the kind who never has to go on a helicopter. And I bet she'll be a stronger person because of what she's lost today. I have a feeling that once you live through something like this, you become a little bit invincible.

I know that makes me a bit of a hypocrite. If that's the case, shouldn't *I* stay? Soldier through it? Maybe if I'd had some practice, maybe if I'd had more devastation in my life, I would be more prepared to go on. It's not that my life has been perfect. I've had disappointments and I've been lonely and frustrated and angry and all the crappy stuff everyone feels. But in terms of heartbreak, I've been spared. I've never toughened up enough to handle what I'd have to handle if I were to stay.

Kim is now telling me about being rescued from certain incarceration by Willow. As she describes how Willow took charge of the whole hospital, there is such admiration in her voice. I picture Kim and Willow becoming friends, even though there are twenty years between them. It makes me happy to imagine them drinking tea or going to the movies together, still connected to each other by the invisible chain of a family that no longer exists.

Now Kim is listing all the people who are at the hospital or who have been, during the course of the day, ticking them off with her fingers: "Your grandparents and aunts, uncles, and cousins. Adam and Brooke Vega and the various rabble-rousers who came with her. Adam's bandmates Mike and Fitzy and Liz and her girlfriend, Sarah, all of whom have been downstairs in the waiting room since they got heaved out of the ICU. Professor Christie, who drove down and stayed half the night before driving back so she could sleep a few hours and shower and make some morning appointment she had. Henry and the baby, who are on their way over right now because the baby woke up at five in the morning and Henry called us and said that he could not stay at home any longer. And me and Mom," Kim concludes. "Shoot. I lost count of how many people that was. But it was a lot. And more have called and asked to come, but your aunt Diane told them to wait. She says that we're making enough nuisance of ourselves. And I think by 'us,' she means me and Adam." Kim stops and smiles for a split second. Then she makes this funny noise, a cross between a cough and a throat-clearing. I've heard her make this sound before; it's what she does when she's summoning her courage, getting ready to jump off the rocks and into the bracing river water.

"I do have a point to all this," she continues. "There are like twenty people in that waiting room right now. Some of them are related to you. Some of them are not. But we're all your family."

She stops now. Leans over me so that the wisps of her hair tickle my face. She kisses me on the forehead. *"You still have a family,"* she whispers.

Last summer, we hosted an accidental Labor Day party at our house. It had been a busy season. Camp for me. Then we'd gone to Gran's family's Massachusetts retreat. I felt like I had barely seen Adam and Kim all summer. My parents were lamenting that they hadn't seen Willow and Henry and the baby in months. "Henry says she's starting to walk," Dad noted that morning. We were all sitting in the living room in front of the fan, trying not to melt. Oregon was having a record heat wave. It was ten in the morning and pushing ninety degrees.

Mom looked up at the calendar. "She's ten months old already. Where has the time gone?" Then she looked at Teddy and me. "How is it humanly possible that I have a daughter who's starting her senior year in high school? How in the hell can my baby boy be starting second grade?"

"I'm not a baby," Teddy shot back, clearly insulted.

"Sorry, kid, unless we have another one, you'll always be my baby."

"Another one?" Dad asked with mock alarm.

"Relax. I'm kidding—for the most part," Mom said. "Let's see how I feel when Mia leaves for college."

"I'm gonna be eight in December. Then I'm a man

and you'll have to call me 'Ted,'" Teddy reported.

"Is that so?" I laughed, spraying orange juice through my nose.

"That's what Casey Carson told me," Teddy said, his mouth set into a determined line.

My parents and I groaned. Casey Carson was Teddy's best friend, and we all liked him a lot and thought his parents seemed like such nice people, so we didn't get how they could give their child such a ridiculous name.

"Well, if Casey Carson says so," I said, giggling, and soon Mom and Dad were laughing, too.

"What's so funny?" Teddy demanded.

"Nothing, Little Man," Dad said. "It's just the heat."

"Can we still do sprinklers today?" Teddy asked. Dad had promised him he could run through the sprinklers that afternoon even though the governor had asked everyone in the state to conserve water this summer. That request had peeved Dad, who claimed that we Oregonians suffer eight months of rain a year and should be exempt from ever worrying about water conservation.

"Damn straight you can," Dad said. "Flood the place if you want."

Teddy seemed placated. "If the baby can walk,

then she can walk through the sprinklers. Can she come into the sprinklers with me?"

Mom looked at Dad. "That's not a bad idea," she said. "I think Willow's off today."

"We could have a barbecue," Dad said. "It *is* Labor Day and grilling in this heat would certainly qualify as labor."

"Plus, we've got a freezer full of steaks from when your father decided to order that side of beef," Mom said. "Why not?"

"Can Adam come?" I asked.

"Of course," Mom said. "We haven't seen much of your young man lately."

"I know," I said. "Things are starting to happen for the band." At the time I was excited about it. Genuinely and completely. Gran had only recently planted the seed of Juilliard in my head, but it hadn't taken root. I hadn't decided to apply yet. Things with Adam had not gotten weird yet.

"If the rock star can handle a humble picnic with squares like us," Dad joked.

"If he can handle a square like me, he can handle squares like you," I joked back. "I think I'll invite Kim, too."

"The more the merrier," Mom said. "We'll make it a blowout like in the olden days."

"When dinosaurs roamed the earth?" Teddy asked.

"Exactly," Dad said. "When dinosaurs roamed the earth and your mom and I were young."

About twenty people showed up. Henry, Willow, the baby, Adam, who brought Fitzy, Kim, who brought a cousin visiting from New Jersey, plus a whole bunch of friends of my parents whom they had not seen in ages. Dad hauled our ancient barbecue out of the basement and spent the afternoon scrubbing it. We grilled up steaks and, this being Oregon, tofu pups and veggie burgers. There was watermelon, which we kept cool in a bucket of ice, and a salad made with vegetables from the organic farm that some of Mom and Dad's friends had started. Mom and I made three pies with wild blackberries that Teddy and I had picked. We drank Pepsi out of these old-fashioned bottles that Dad had found at some ancient country store, and I swear they tasted better than the regular kind. Maybe it was because it was so hot, or that the party was so last minute, or maybe because everything tastes better on the grill, but it was one of those meals that you know you'll remember.

When Dad turned on the sprinkler for Teddy

and the baby, everyone else decided to run through it. We left it on so long that the brown grass turned into a big slippery puddle and I wondered if the governor himself might come and tell us off. Adam tackled me and we laughed and squirmed around on the lawn. It was so hot, I didn't bother changing into dry clothes, just kept dousing myself whenever I got too sweaty. By the end of the day, my sundress was stiff. Teddy had taken his shirt off and had streaked himself with mud. Dad said he looked like one of the boys from *Lord of the Flies*.

When it started to get dark, most people left to catch the fireworks display at the university or to see a band called Oswald Five-0 play in town. A handful of people, including Adam, Kim, Willow, and Henry, stayed. When it cooled off, Dad lit a campfire on the lawn, and we roasted marshmallows. Then the musical instruments appeared. Dad's snare drum from the house, Henry's guitar from his car, Adam's spare guitar from my room. Everyone was jamming together, singing songs: Dad's songs, Adam's songs, old Clash songs, old Wipers songs. Teddy was dancing around, the blond of his hair reflecting the golden flames. I remember watching it all and getting that tickling in my chest and thinking to myself: *This is what happiness feels like.*

At one point, Dad and Adam stopped playing and I caught them whispering about something. Then they went inside, to get more beer, they claimed. But when they returned they were carrying my cello.

"Oh, no, I'm not giving a concert," I said.

"We don't want you to," Dad said. "We want you to play with us."

"No way," I said. Adam had occasionally tried to get me to "jam" with him and I always refused. Lately he'd started joking about us playing air-guitar–air-cello duets, which was about as far as I was willing to go.

"Why not, Mia?" Kim said. "Are you such a classical-music snob?"

"It's not that," I said, suddenly feeling panicked. "It's just that the two styles don't fit together."

"Says who?" Mom asked, her eyebrows raised.

"Yeah, who knew you were such a musical seg-regationist?" Henry joked.

Willow rolled her eyes at Henry and turned to me. "Pretty please," she said as she rocked the baby to sleep in her lap. "I never get to hear you play anymore."

"C'mon, Mee," Henry said. "You're among family."

"Totally," Kim said.

Adam took my hand and caressed the inside of my wrist with his fingers. "Do it for me. I really want to play with you. Just once."

I was about to shake my head, to reaffirm that my cello had no place among the jamming guitars, no place in the punk-rock world. But then I looked out at Mom, who was smirking at me, as if issuing a challenge, and Dad, who was tapping on his pipe, pretending to be nonchalant so as not to apply any pressure, and Teddy, who was jumping up and down—though I think it was because he was hopped up on marshmallows, not because he had any desire to hear me play—and Kim and Willow and Henry all peering at me like this really mattered, and Adam, looking as awed and proud as he always did when he listened to me play. And I was a little scared of falling on my face, of not blending, of making bad music. But everyone was looking at me so intently, wanting me to join in so much, and I realized that sounding bad wasn't the worst thing in the world that could happen.

So I played. And even though you wouldn't think it, the cello didn't sound half bad with all those guitars. In fact, it sounded pretty amazing.

———

It's morning. And inside the hospital, there's a different kind of dawn, a rustling of covers, a clearing of the eyes. In some ways, the hospital never goes to sleep. The lights stay on and the nurses stay awake, but even though it's still dark outside, you can tell that things are waking up. The doctors are back, yanking on my eyelids, shining their lights at me, frowning as they scribble notes in my chart as though I've let them down.

I don't care anymore. I'm tired of this all, and it will be over soon. The social worker is back on duty again, too. It looks like the night's sleep had little impact on her. Her eyes are still heavy, her hair a kinky mess. She reads my chart and listens to updates from the nurses on my bumpy night, which seems to make her even more tired. The nurse with the blue-black skin is also back. She greeted me by telling me how glad she was to see me this morning, how she'd been thinking about me last night, hoping I'd be here. Then she noticed the bloodstain on my blanket and *tsked tsked* before hustling off to get me a new one.

After Kim left, there haven't been any more visitors. I guess Willow has run out of people to lobby me with. I wonder if this deciding business is something that *all* the nurses are aware of. Nurse Ramirez sure knew about it. And I think the nurse with me now knows it, too, judging by how congratulatory she's acting that I made it through the night. And Willow seems like she knows it, too, with the way she's been marching everyone through here. I like these nurses so much. I hope they will not take my decision personally.

I am so tired now that I can barely blink my eyes. It's all just a matter of time, and part of me wonders why I'm delaying the inevitable. But I know why. I'm waiting for Adam to come back. Though it seems like he has been gone for an eternity, it's probably only been an hour. And he asked me to wait, so I will. That's the least I can do for him.

My eyes are closed so I hear him before I see him. I hear the raspy, quick rushes of his lungs. He is panting like he just ran a marathon. Then I smell the sweat on him, a clean musky scent that I'd bottle and wear as perfume if I could. I open my eyes. Adam has closed his. But the lids are puffy and pink, so I know what he's been doing. Is that why he went away? To cry without my seeing?

He doesn't so much sit in the chair as fall into

it, like clothes heaped onto the floor at the end of a long day. He covers his face with his hands and takes deep breaths to steady himself. After a minute, he drops his hands into his lap. "Just listen," he says with a voice that sounds like shrapnel.

I open my eyes wide now. I sit up as much as I can. And I listen.

"Stay." With that one word, Adam's voice catches, but he swallows the emotion and pushes forward. "There's no word for what happened to you. There's no good side of it. But there *is* something to live for. And I'm not talking about me. It's just . . . I don't know. Maybe I'm talking shit. I know I'm in shock. I know I haven't digested what happened to your parents, to Teddy . . . " When he says Teddy, his voice cracks and an avalanche of tears tumbles down his face. And I think: *I love you.*

I hear him take gulpfuls of air to steady himself. And then he continues: "All I can think about is how fucked up it would be for your life to end here, now. I mean, I know that your life is fucked up no matter what now, forever. And I'm not dumb enough to think that I can undo that, that anyone can. But I can't wrap my mind around the notion of you not getting old, having kids, going to Juilliard, getting to play that cello in front of a huge audience, so that they can get the chills the way I do every time I see you pick up your bow, every time I see you smile at me.

"If you stay, I'll do whatever you want. I'll quit the band, go with you to New York. But if you need me to go away, I'll do that, too. I was talking to Liz and she said maybe coming back to your old life would just be too painful, that maybe it'd be easier for you to erase us. And that would suck, but I'd do it. I can lose you like that if I don't lose you today. I'll let you go. If you stay."

Then it is Adam who lets go. His sobs burst like fists pounding against tender flesh.

I close my eyes. I cover my ears. I cannot watch this. I cannot hear this.

But then, it is no longer Adam that I hear. It's that sound, the low moan that in an instant takes flight and turns into something sweet. It's the cello. Adam has placed headphones over my lifeless ears and is laying an iPod down on my chest. He's apologizing, saying that he knows this isn't my favorite but it was the best he could do. He turns up the volume so I can hear the music floating across the morning air. Then he takes my hand.

It is Yo-Yo Ma. Playing *Andante con moto e poco rubato*. The low piano plays almost as if in warning.

In comes the cello, like a heart bleeding. And it's like something inside of me implodes.

I am sitting around the breakfast table with my family, drinking hot coffee, laughing at Teddy's chocolate-chip mustache. The snow is blowing outside.

I am visiting a cemetery. Three graves under a tree on a hill overlooking the river.

I am lying with Adam, my head on his chest, on a sandy bank next to the river.

I am hearing people say the word *orphan* and realize that they're talking about me.

I am walking through New York City with Kim, the skyscrapers casting shadows on our faces.

I am holding Teddy on my lap, tickling him as he giggles so hard he keels over.

I am sitting with my cello, the one Mom and Dad gave me after my first recital. My fingers caress the wood and the pegs, which time and touch have worn smooth. My bow is poised over the strings now. I am looking at my hand, waiting to start playing.

I am looking at my hand, being held by Adam's hand.

Yo-Yo Ma continues to play, and it's like the piano and cello are being poured into my body, the same way that the IV and blood transfusions are. And the memories of my life as it was, and the flashes of it as it might be, are coming so fast and furious. I feel like I can no longer keep up with them but they keep coming and everything is colliding, until I cannot take it anymore. Until I cannot be like this one second longer.

There is a blinding flash, a pain that rips through me for one searing instant, a silent scream from my broken body. For the first time, I can sense how fully agonizing staying will be.

But then I feel Adam's hand. Not sense it, but feel it. I'm not sitting huddled in the chair anymore. I'm lying on my back in the hospital bed, one again with my body.

Adam is crying and somewhere inside of me I am crying, too, because I'm feeling things at last. I'm feeling not just the physical pain, but all that I have lost, and it is profound and catastrophic and will leave a crater in me that nothing will ever fill. But I'm also feeling all that I have in my life, which includes what I have lost, as well as the great unknown of what life might still bring me. And it's all too much. The feelings pile up, threatening to crack my chest wide-open. The only way to survive them is to concentrate on Adam's hand. Grasping mine.

And suddenly I just *need* to hold his hand more than I've ever needed anything in this world. Not just be held by it, but hold it back. I aim every remaining ounce of energy into my right hand. I'm weak, and this is so hard. It's the hardest thing I will ever have to do. I summon all the love I have ever felt, I summon all the strength that Gran and Gramps and Kim and the nurses and Willow have given me. I summon all the breath that Mom, Dad, and Teddy would fill me with if they could. I summon all my own strength, focus it like a laser beam into the fingers and palm of my right hand. I picture my hand stroking Teddy's hair, grasping a bow poised above my cello, interlaced with Adam's.

And then I squeeze.

I slump back, spent, unsure of whether I just did what I did. Of what it means. If it registered. If it matters.

But then I feel Adam's grip tighten, so that the grasp of his hand feels like it is holding my entire body. Like it could lift me up right out of this bed. And then I hear the sharp intake of his breath followed by the sound of his voice. It's the first time today I can truly hear him.

"Mia?" he asks.

ACKNOWLEDGMENTS

Several people came together in a short amount of time to make *If I Stay* possible. It starts with Gillian Aldrich, who started crying (in a good way) when I told her about my idea. This proved to be quite a good motivator to get started.

Tamara Glenny, Eliza Griswold, Kim Sevcik, and Sean Smith took time out of their hectic schedules to read early drafts and offer much-needed encouragement. For their enduring generosity and friendship, I love and thank them. Some people help you keep your head straight; Marjorie Ingall helps me keep my heart straight, and for that I love and thank her. Thank you also to Jana and Moshe Banin.

Sarah Burnes is my agent in the truest sense of the word,

harnessing her formidable intelligence, insight, passion, and warmth to shepherd the words that I write to the people who should read them. She and the superb Courtney Gatewood and Stephanie Cabot have made miracles happen where this book is concerned.

When I first met with the team at Penguin, I felt like I was sitting down with family. My extraordinary editor, Julie Strauss-Gabel, has lavished Mia and her family (not to mention me) with the careful attention and love you'd hope to get from a relative. She is "Julie-special." Don Weisberg put both heart and muscle into this book, and the editorial, sales, marketing, publicity, and design people have all gone above and beyond, and for that I want to individually thank: Heather Alexander, Emilie Bandy, Monica Benalcazar, Scottie Bowditch, Leigh Butler, Mary-Margaret Callahan, Lisa DeGroff, Erin Dempsey, Jackie Engel, Felicia Frazier, Jana Fruh, Kristin Gilson, Jennifer Haller, Lauri Hornik, Annie Hurwitz, RasShahn Johnson-Baker, Deborah Kaplan, Melanie Klesse, Eileen Kreit, Kimberly Lauber, Rosanne Lauer, Stephanie Owens Lurie, Andrea Mai, Gerard Mancini, Barbara Marcus, Mary McGrath, Casey McIntyre, Steve Meltzer, Shanta Newlin, Patti Pirooz, Leslie Prives, Lydah Pyles, Mary Raymond, Chadd Reese, Emily Romero, Holly Ruck, Stephanie Sabol, Jana Singer, Natalie Sousa, Ev Taylor, Laurence Tucci, Allison Verost, Allan Winebarger, Courtney Wood, Heather Wood, and Lisa Yoskowitz. And finally a huge thank-you to the field reps who worked so hard on behalf of this book. (Phew.)

Music is a huge part of this story, and I drew a lot of inspiration from Yo-Yo Ma—whose own work informs much of Mia's story—and from Glen Hansard and Marketa Irglova, whose song "Falling Slowly" I probably listened to more than two hundred times while working on the book.

Thanks to my Oregon contingent: Greg and Diane Rios, who have been our compatriots through all this. John and Peg Christie, whose grace, dignity, and generosity continue to move me. Jennifer Larson, M.D., an old friend and, as luck would have it an emergency room doctor, who enlightened me about Glasgow Coma Scales, among other medical details.

My parents—Lee and Ruth Forman—and my siblings—Tamar Schamhart and Greg Forman—are my cheerleaders and most steadfast fans, who ignore my failings (professional ones, anyhow) and celebrate my successes as if they were their own (which they are). Thank you also to Karen Forman, Robert Schamhart, and Detta Tucker.

I didn't immediately recognize how much of this book is about the way parents transform their lives for their children. Willa Tucker teaches me this lesson every day and is occasionally forgiving when I am too absorbed playing make-believe in my head to play make-believe with her.

Without my husband, Nick Tucker, none of this would be. I owe him everything.

Finally, my deepest thanks go to R.D.T.J., who inspire me in so many ways and who show me every single day that there is such a thing as immortality.

**KEEP READING FOR
A NEVER-BEFORE-PUBLISHED
SPECIAL PREQUEL TO *IF I STAY*!**

PROPHECY

She was done with guys. She really was.

"I'm done with guys," she announced to Heather as they scrubbed out an industrial-size vat of macaroni and cheese.

They had known each other since freshman year when they'd randomly been assigned to the same shitty work-study job (washing dishes in the dining hall, the same work-study job they still had) and had spent the last eighteen months trying to erase the previous eighteen years. Such proclamations were part of the process. A way of denouncing the girls they had been, and announcing the women they were willing themselves to become. *I drink coffee black now, they proclaimed. I study philosophy now. I am a feminist now.*

It was like one of those cheesy inspirational quotes. Fake it till you make it.

"You're sure you're not just upset over Cory?" Heather asked, grabbing the pan and hosing it before putting it in the Hobart.

Well, yeah, she was upset over Cory. But he was just a symptom of a disease known as dickhood. Cory, who had chased her, wooed her, left flowers on her doorstep, and then, after they'd hooked up, had avoided her like she had leprosy. It was all or nothing. Guys were either possessive, wanting to consume every ounce of you, or dismissive, throwing you away like a used Kleenex.

It had been this way since she was thirteen, when she'd first grown breasts and hips and emitted pheromones that made the boys whistle as she walked home from school. That made her own stepfather look at her with wolfish eyes.

Guys were the one thing she could not seem to demarcate. They had always been assholes. They would always be assholes, only instead of being assholes named Trent whose idea of a romantic night was a six-pack in the bed of a truck, now the assholes were named Dylan, whose idea of a romantic night was having her gaze adoringly at him as he performed at poetry slams or strummed Dead songs.

Dicks. All of them.

"Maybe it's not you; maybe it's the guys," Heather said. Last year, Heather had really departed from her previous self by sleeping with girls. She said she wasn't sure what it meant yet, only that it was fun. And very different.

Very different appealed to her, but the one time she'd kissed Heather, just for experimentation's sake, it had felt like kissing, well, her best friend.

"Maybe you should pick guys for me from now on," she suggested to Heather.

"Ohh. Power, I like that," Heather said conspiratorially. She peered out at the dining hall. Dinner was almost over, only the stragglers remaining. "What about that one?" Heather asked, pointing the sink's hose at one guy with long blond dreadlocks.

"White-boy dreadlocks? Pass!"

"Fine," Heather said. "How about that one?" She pointed to a cute guy with shaggy hair that fell over his big thick glasses. "Look, he's smart. He's even reading a book."

"Poseur."

"How can you tell?"

"No one reads in the cafeteria unless they're trying to be seen reading in the cafeteria. I bet the glasses aren't even real. And I bet he's reading something totally assholish."

"You're so cynical. Maybe he's reading for a class. And anyhow, I'm the boss now. Go talk to him."

"Fine."

She hung up her apron on the hook and fluffed her hair, which was stupid, but she did it anyway. She walked into the dining hall, picking up trays the lazier students failed to bring to the belt. She glanced at the guy's book, and kept walking.

"That was fast," Heather said. "What happened?"

"He was reading *Atlas Shrugged.*"

"I hereby resign as your guy consultant."

"I hereby accept your resignation."

He was in his bedroom, making a mixtape. There was an art to it, layering songs and moods, alternating beats and tempo. It wasn't that different from writing lyrics. Or even playing a gig. With his kit around him, he felt like he was in his own universe.

"Whatcha doing?" asked his best friend and bandmate, Henry, poking his head in the doorway.

"Making a mixtape," he said.

Henry came over to inspect the albums he'd culled for the tape. A lot of them were LPs they'd discovered together.

They'd met at freshman orientation, drawn to

each other because they'd both been wearing Ramones T-shirts. Among all the hippies with their tie-dye and batik, it was like finding a secret agent in enemy territory.

"Who else do you like?" Henry had asked him, without preamble, at the orientation mixer.

He'd responded: "Wipers, the Rats, Neo Boys."

"I don't know them. What about SST stuff: Saccharine Trust, Minutemen, Black Flag?"

"Love Black Flag. Don't know Saccharine Trust."

"Oh, man. How have you even lived?"

After that they were off to the races, spending their spare time digging through the bins at Moby Disc, pooling money to buy LPs from Velvet Underground, the Modern Lovers, Radio Birdman, the Stooges, the Saints. He considered this as much a part of his education as Comparative Lit and Intro to Archeology.

They played their albums as loudly as they could on the tiny turntable that Henry had bought at the Goodwill. Not loud enough for them, but loud enough for Henry's roommate to complain, repeatedly, to the RA.

"Next year, let's get our own place," Henry said.

Sophomore year, they'd rented two rooms in a house occupied by two seniors. One of them was a girl named Cara, who used to be part of his sister Diane's posse of good-smelling girls. Back in high school, when he'd spent most of his spare time in his bedroom, reading books, listening to the Ramones, yearning for something unnamable, he used to pine for those girls. They in turn had treated him like the family dog. Cara even used to ruffle his hair. When he'd complained about the indignity of this to his sister, she'd laughed and ruffled his hair, too. "Don't worry," she'd told him. "You're just a late bloomer."

The house's previous tenants had left an old snare drum and an amp that Cara suspected was dead but maybe needed a new fuse. Cara asked them if they wouldn't mind carrying them to the curb for garbage, but instead he and Henry had decided that they'd fix the amp and start a band.

That neither of them knew how to play seemed like a minor detail. They'd get there. They found a bass player and christened the band with a name before they even knew how to play. "It was an act of faith," Henry liked to say.

And he'd been right. Here they were, a year later. A real band. They had a gig that night. But first, he had to finish his tape.

"Are you making that tape for a girl?" Henry asked, waggling his eyebrows ludicrously.

There was no girl. Henry knew that. But Henry

also knew him well. He *was* making the tape for a girl. He just hadn't met her yet.

After she and Heather finished their shift, they went back to the dorm to shower the smell of other people's dinner off and change. It was Thursday night. Their night to go out. Another demarcation, because back home, people stayed in and watched *Cheers.* So here they went out on Thursdays.

"Where do you want to go?" Heather asked.

"Vet's Club, of course," she replied.

The Vet's Club was a dark bar they'd discovered. It served old-timey cocktails, unironically, had a cigarette machine that only charged two bucks for a pack of Lucky Strikes. It was tended by mildly pervy old men in Shriner hats and military uniforms, who, if you wore red lipstick and flirted, didn't ask for ID.

The bar was an odd throwback to the towns they'd grown up in—the men, the outdated uniforms, the currency of sex—but because this made it such an outlier here in their hippie-dippie college town, it qualified as another distinction. They left lipstick smudges on their screwdrivers and cigarettes, as they debated whether flirting with geezers to drink at a place like this constituted exploiting their sexuality, or taking control of it.

No sooner had they slipped into their favorite booth and ordered their favorite drinks than the door swung open. Heather was facing out, and she could see by her face that whoever had just entered was not welcome.

It was Cory. And some new girl, a hippie chick with flowing locks and twinkling ankle brace-lets that seemed to announce that she knew things about sex you could never fathom.

"What's *he* doing here?" Heather asked.

She sipped her screwdriver, miserably.

Heather continued: "Did you bring *Cory* to our place?"

She hung her head in shame. She had, stupidly eager to show him all her favorite places. And now he had taken another girl here. She was humiliated anew.

Why did she keep doing that? Why did she give away all the secret parts of herself to other people when they would only squander them on girls with anklets?

They left without finishing their drinks.

"Are you okay?" Heather asked her as they emerged into the misty night.

She wasn't okay; Heather knew this. But both understood how to say things without speaking of them. Neither had talked much about their lives before college, neither had shared horror stories about their fathers and stepfathers, about late night visits from the cops, about rows of empty bottles of Jack on kitchen countertops. They didn't need to talk so much as be understood.

"Cory doesn't get to ruin our night," Heather declared. "He's not worthy."

Fucking Cory. She didn't even like him that much. He was another pretty patchouli boy with big eyes and soft lips. But the more she read Virginia Woolf or Angela Davis, the more she learned about matriarchal societies in China or how Moroccan women exercised authority behind the closed doors of their purdah, the more she felt herself growing away from her small, unhappy life at home.

But then she'd spend a night with a Cory, or Dylan, or Geoff, and things would be absolutely no different than they'd been before with a Trent or Billy Bob or Jeff. It yanked her back. It made her doubt she would ever truly escape.

As they rode their bikes away from the bar, it began to rain. It was always raining here, but tonight the rain felt different: soft and warm and somehow cleansing, like a baptism. Maybe that was what she needed. Not an actual baptism (she'd had one of those as a kid) but a spiritual one. Something to truly extinguish the person she would've become had she stayed home—the one her mom and her sister and her aunts already were—from the person she wanted to be.

The remark she'd made earlier about giving up guys came back to her. Only this time it didn't feel like a joke.

"I saw you play at Bozo Lounge the other night," said a girl, Rebecca, he thought her name was. She touched him gently on the shoulder. "You were so fucking good."

"Thanks," he said, looking around for Henry, who had borrowed his latest girl's car to haul their gear over. He was late. What else was new?

"I really liked the last song, the long churning one with the guitar solo." She smiled and touched him on the shoulder again.

"Thanks," he replied. The song, "Cutaway," was his. He'd written it a few weeks before. It was his best track yet.

Last year, when the band first started playing, they only did covers, Ramones, the Clash, the Replacements. It was blatant mimicry, but it was the most they could do. Henry could only play three chords, and he could barely manage a 4/4 time with no fills. The bass player they'd picked up, a sophmore named Billie, had played bass for a mandated year in her high school's orchestra. To say they sucked was generous.

With a punk-rock bravado, they played out anyway. No one laughed them off the stage (or what passed as a stage in a house-party basement). The other music nerds in town found their lack of polish a badge of honor, an antidote to the slickness of contemporary music. Henry learned barre chords. Billie learned bass runs. He mastered quarter notes. They started writing their own songs. They became a real band. They became part of a scene.

A scene that included girls. Once he had a pair of sticks in his hands, they were everywhere.

Like here, now. Rebecca had been joined by another girl named Lindsey who was presently asking him if the band was going to record.

"We just cut a single," he said, wanting to get out of here. Where was Henry?

"Right, I read about that in the interview you did," Rebecca said. "I loved the bit about how you were a drummer before you knew it." She turned to Lindsey. "He used to drum along to Ramones tracks with pencils."

He had done that. In high school. On a pillow.

He hadn't even realized he was doing it until his mom came and asked what was happening to all her pillowcases.

"I didn't see that interview," Lindsey said. "Where was it?"

Rebecca named the zine. "It was a two-page spread, calling these guys the next Gun Club."

"Really? I think the sound is more like X. With Billie and Henry singing."

"Billie's singing has a raw feel. Reminds me of Patti Smith," Rebecca said.

"You're so right. I love Patti Smith," Lindsey said.

"Me too," Rebecca said.

Now *they* were off to the races, and he was glad for them. They were no longer interested in him, and he was glad for that, too.

If Henry were here, he'd smack him. "We're like foxes who've been invited into the henhouse and now you decide to be a vegetarian." Henry took full advantage of his new status as rock god to hook up with as many girls as possible.

But he had joined a band for the music, for the friendship, not for the girls. Which wasn't to say he wasn't interested in them. He hadn't forgotten the way his sister's friends had smelled, how he'd closed his eyes, breathed them in, and yearned.

He'd even gotten together with Cara, one of the good-smelling girls. It didn't last.

"You're an asshole," Cara had fumed when he'd broken it off after a few weeks.

He wasn't trying to be an asshole. He was trying to be honest. And the truth was, every time he got together with a girl, it didn't lessen his yearning; it deepened it.

Maybe he was an asshole. Or deluded to think that any girl could satisfy his yearning. Maybe love was a construct, something dreamed up so musicians had something to write songs about.

Except he had a whole shoebox full of mixtapes he intended to give to someone, someday. He had the tape he'd made earlier that afternoon in his Walkman. Those tapes were a declaration. They were an act of faith.

He excused himself from Lindsey and Rebecca. He put on his Walkman. He listened to his latest creation and read a book until Henry showed up and it was time to load in.

"Hey, Heather," she called as they rode their bikes through the mist. "Maybe I should give up guys after all." Not forever, but for a distinct period of time. A year.

But Heather didn't hear her. She was pedaling ahead, lured by the sound of amplified music coming out of a blue-and-white craftsman cottage. The house was all lit up, like a beacon on the otherwise dark, quiet street.

"What is this place?" she asked when she'd caught up with Heather.

"I don't know. But we should find out."

She stayed with the bikes while Heather went in to investigate. The night was beginning to take on a surreal air. The Vet's Club, Cory, felt like hours—no, days—ago. It was like they'd ridden their bikes into a different country.

Heather returned from her reconnaissance mission stating the obvious. "It's a bunch of bands playing," she said. She held up a flyer. None of the names were familiar.

Neither was the music, loud and churning, raw and somehow fully formed. It was a far cry from the Madonna or Dead tunes that piped through the dorm.

It was different. Everything about the house was different, from the people playing chess on the porch to the girls unselfconsciously pogoing on the sidewalk. To the guy leaning against the basement door, reading a book. Unlike the poseur in the cafeteria, who seemed to be performing the act of reading, this guy seemed to be lost in the pages.

She studied him. She didn't think she'd seen him before—the university's student body was twice the size of her hometown's population—but he seemed familiar. She wondered what book had him so rapt.

She could go up to him and ask. He would answer. The guys always did with her.

But then she remembered the vow she'd made just minutes before, if it even qualified as a vow yet. No one knew about it, not even Heather. She wasn't sure she'd go through with it.

But she also wasn't sure she wouldn't.

She decided to leave. Maybe she would come back another time. Maybe he would still be here.

She kissed Heather on the cheek, lipstick leaving a mark. Told her to have fun for the both of them. Then she got on her bike and rode back to the dorm.

The tape ended and he flipped it over. The first track on Side 2 was from the Modern Lovers, an album Henry had introduced him to. He'd chosen the song "Girlfriend." He liked how Jonathan Richman sang about his desire, his aching need to have someone to walk hand in hand with, someone to understand, in a voice so full of longing that he would've understood what Jonathan was singing about even if the song had been in Japanese.

He looked up and there was a girl nearby, holding the handlebars of a bike, watching him. She looked like the other girls, pretty, red lipstick. Except her eyes. There was a ferocity to them. Like a bear, protecting her turf.

When he looked up again, the girl with the ferocious eyes had ridden away.

That night, she had the strangest dream. She dreamed about the boy with the book. They were sitting in a house, in front of a fireplace, with kids. And he was reading a book again, and she kept trying to see which one it was, only she couldn't because you could never see books in dreams.

She woke up. The dream was like a window, one that offered a glimpse of a kind of happiness, one she had neither witnessed nor experienced, but believed, on faith, existed. She wanted to climb through that window, live in that dream, to will that cozy tableau into being.

She did not wake Heather, or go to the dining hall for breakfast, or do any of the things she normally did on Friday mornings. Instead, she skipped class and took a walk through the cemetery near campus. It was peaceful there. It let her think.

By the time she left the cemetery, she was resolved. She would give up guys for a year. The dream she'd had somehow cemented this.

The resolution brought her a profound sense of relief and then a giddy sort of joy. She decided to celebrate with a coffee and a muffin from her favorite café.

The night before, ears still ringing from the gig, he played his new tape again, partly to make sure the songs were all working in harmony, partly to drown out the sounds Henry was making with the latest girl.

The "Girlfriend" song came on again. "G-I-R-L-F-R-E-N," Jonathan sang.

Maybe it was the goofy spelling or Henry's hijinks, but it suddenly struck him that *girlfriend* was such a stupid word. It sounded so trivial. What he wanted, what he suspected Jonathan wanted, was something deeper than that. Something more substantial.

But he didn't know what that was. He fell asleep not knowing and woke up not knowing, and as he made his way to campus, stopping for a coffee, he still did not know.

When she saw him sitting in front of Café Roma, she wasn't surprised, even though she had never seen him here before.

He sat on the curb, coffee next to him, Chuck Taylors spackled with leaves of wet grass. He was scribbling in a little book. Again, she was struck that he was fully engaged in what he was doing. He didn't care if he was being watched.

He was being watched.

The dream returned to her, so real, so palpable, she could've sworn it was prophecy.

She wanted to tell him about the dream. After all, it was his family, too. Their family.

Which was insane.

She decided to administer a test. If he passed, she'd tell him. If he failed, she would not.

She waited until he finished writing whatever it was he'd been writing, and put the little book away.

"Excuse me," she said, sitting down next to him. "I know this is a strange question, but what book were you reading last night?"

He looked at her a long time before answering. And then he methodically went through his bag, pulling out a Walkman, a wallet, and finally a book. She girded herself, hoping it would not be something awful like Ayn Rand or Jack Kerouac.

He handed her the book.

Looking back on this moment, she would swear she had heard the sound of a bell ringing, though she couldn't figure out where it would've come from.

The book was *The Hound of the Baskervilles*. She remembered when the librarian in her town had first given her a Sherlock Holmes book. Eighth grade. No one read at her house, so this was the first time she'd ever gotten truly lost in a book. What a revelation, that there could be worlds within words. Sensing her hunger, the librarian had fed her the whole series. Four years later, when she decided to apply to college, the librarian had helped her with the applications and financial-aid forms.

"That's one of my favorite books," she said. And then she told him her dream.

He had not been surprised to see her, either, even though he had not ever recalled seeing her at this café before.

Nor was he surprised when she asked what book he was reading. Or when she said that it was her favorite.

Then she told him about her dream. Them, together, in the future. With kids.

Okay, here he was a little surprised.

But then he thought of Jonathan Richman, his inchoate longing. And he understood what it was he was looking for, not a girlfriend but a wife, a family. What his parents had.

"Were we married?" he asked her.

"Yes," she replied. "We were married."

She had embarrassed herself, she could feel the heat creeping up her neck, but he seemed unperturbed. He was making none of those sidestepping remarks to get the hell away, none of the kind of stuttered excuses that Cory or Dylan would've offered. As soon as the thought crossed her mind, she banished it. She did not want to think of Cory or Dylan anymore.

"You want to go get a coffee?" he said, gesturing toward the café.

"I'd love to," she said.

And then her stomach bottomed out as everything came together. The vow was connected to the dream. The dream would not happen without keeping the vow.

"But I can't."

She explained why.

He absorbed the news quietly, thoughtfully. "A year," he said at last.

She would've said something about not expecting him to wait for her, except that seemed more than a little presumptuous.

He pulled out his book, the one he'd been scribbling in. "What's the date today?" he asked.

She told him.

He uncapped his pen and wrote down the date. But then, instead of 1988, which it was, he wrote 1989. He encased the date in a black square. To make it official.

"We'll have coffee then," he said.

She stared at him like she didn't believe him.

"Are you serious?"

He was as serious as a heart attack. As serious as love. "I'm serious," he told her.

"You don't know me. And you might find someone else."

"I won't."

"For a whole year?"

"What's a year in a life if it's a happy life?" He paused. "Is it a happy life?"

She had no way of knowing this to be true. Only that it was.

"Yes," she told him. "We are really happy."

He closed his book and put it back into his bag. He put the Walkman back, too. The tape was inside it. It belonged to her. When they met for coffee one year from today, he would give all the tapes he'd made to her. They'd keep. Music was eternal like that.

She handed him back the Doyle, but he shook his head. "Keep it until next year," he said.

A year. She would take the year to grow and heal and educate herself, and make herself ready for the life that she wanted. A life that she deserved.

"Should we shake on it or something?" she asked him.

When they shook hands, any remaining doubt he had disappeared. This was a hand he'd walk down the aisle grasping, a hand that would squeeze his like a vise as their children entered the world.

They shook a long time, giving themselves this moment to hold hands under the auspices of sealing a deal. Neither wanted to let go. A year was a long time. But he was right. Not long in a life.

They let go. She stood to leave and then remembered something important. "What's your name?"

"I'm Denny."

"Denny," she repeated. The name already felt familiar on her tongue, a language she'd understood since birth.

"I'm Kat," she said.

Kat. He saw himself introducing her to his parents, his family.

He saw it all roll out in front of him.

They both did.

THREE YEARS LATER,
MIA AND ADAM'S STORY
CONTINUES IN . . .

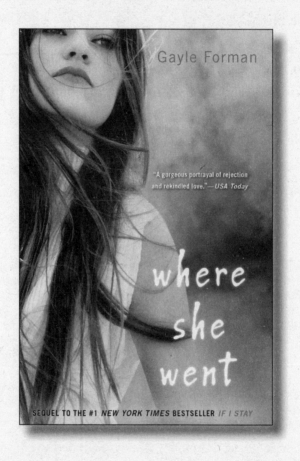

Gayle Forman

"A gorgeous portrayal of rejection
and rekindled love."—*USA Today*

where
she
went

SEQUEL TO THE #1 *NEW YORK TIMES* BESTSELLER *IF I STAY*

THREE

Mia woke up after four days, but we didn't tell her until the sixth day. It didn't matter because she seemed to already know. We sat around her hospital bed in the ICU, her taciturn grandfather having drawn the short straw, I guess, because he was the one chosen to break the news that her parents, Kat and Denny, had been killed instantly in the car crash that had landed her here. And that her little brother, Teddy, had died in the emergency room of the local hospital where he and Mia had been brought to before Mia was evacuated to Portland.

Nobody knew the cause of the crash. Did Mia have any memory of it?

Mia just lay there, blinking her eyes and holding onto my hand, digging her nails in so tightly it seemed like she'd never let me go. She shook her head and quietly said "no, no, no," over and over again, but without tears, and I wasn't sure if she was answering her grandfather's question or just negating the whole situation. *No!*

But then the social worker stepped in, taking over in her no-nonsense way. She told Mia about the operations she'd undergone so far, "triage, really, just to get you stable, and you're doing remarkably well," and then talked about the surgeries that she'd likely be facing in the coming months: First a surgery to reset the bone in her left leg with metal rods. Then another surgery a week or so after that, to harvest skin from the thigh of her uninjured leg. Then another to graft that skin onto the messed-up leg. Those two procedures, unfortunately, would leave some "nasty scars." But the injuries on her face, at least, could vanish completely with cosmetic surgery after a year. "Once you're through your nonelective surgeries, provided there aren't any complications—no infections from the splenectomy, no pneumonia, no problems with your lungs—we'll get you out of the hospital and into rehab," the social worker said. "Physical and occupational, speech and whatever else you need. We'll assess where you are in a few days." I was dizzy from this litany, but Mia seemed to hang on her every word, to pay more attention to the details of her surgeries than to the news of her family.

Later that afternoon, the social worker took the rest of us aside. We—Mia's grandparents and me—had been worried about Mia's reaction, or her lack of one. We'd expected screaming, hair pulling, something explosive, to match the horror of the news, to match our *own* grief. Her eerie quiet had all of us thinking the same thing: brain damage.

"No, that's not it," the social worker quickly reassured. "The brain is a fragile instrument and we may not know for a few weeks what specific regions have been affected, but young people are so very resilient and right now her neurologists are quite optimistic. Her motor control is generally good. Her language faculties don't seem too affected. She has weakness in her right side and her balance is off. If that's the extent of her brain injury, then she is fortunate."

We all cringed at that word. *Fortunate.* But the social worker looked at our faces. "*Very* fortunate because all of that is reversible. As for that reaction back there," she said, gesturing toward the ICU, "that is a typical response to such extreme psychological trauma. The brain can only handle so much, so it filters in a bit at a time,

digests slowly. She'll take it all in, but she'll need help."
Then she'd told us about the stages of grief, loaded us
up with pamphlets on post-traumatic stress disorder, and
recommended a grief counselor at the hospital for Mia
to see. "It might not be a bad idea for the rest of you,
too," she'd said.

We'd ignored her. Mia's grandparents weren't the
therapy types. And as for me, I had Mia's rehabilitation
to worry about, not my own.

The next round of surgeries started almost immediately, which I found cruel. Mia had just come back from
the brink of it, only to be told her family was dead, and
now she had to go under the knife again. Couldn't they
cut the girl a break? But the social worker had explained
that the sooner Mia's leg was fixed, the sooner Mia
would be mobile, and the sooner she could really start
to heal. So her femur was set with pins; skin grafts were
taken. And with speed that made me breathless, she was
discharged from the hospital and dispatched to a rehab
center, which looked like a condo complex, with flat
paths crisscrossing the grounds, which were just beginning to bloom with spring flowers when Mia arrived.

She'd been there less than a week, a determined,
teeth-gritted terrifying week, when the envelope came.

Juilliard. It had been so many things to me before.
A foregone conclusion. A point of pride. A rival. And

then I'd just forgotten about it. I think we all had. But life was churning outside Mia's rehab center, and somewhere out there in the world, that other Mia—the one who had two parents, a brother, and a fully working body—still continued to exist. And in that other world, some judges had listened to Mia play a few months earlier and had gone on processing her application, and it had gone through the various motions until a final judgment was made, and that final judgment was before us now. Mia's grandmother had been too nervous to open the envelope, so she waited for me and Mia's grandfather before she sliced into it with a mother-of-pearl letter opener.

Mia got in. Had there ever been any question?

We all thought the acceptance would be good for her, a bright spot on an otherwise bleak horizon.

"And I've already spoken to the dean of admissions and explained your situation, and they've said you can put off starting for a year, two if you need," Mia's grandmother had said as she'd presented Mia with the news and the generous scholarship that had accompanied the acceptance. Juilliard had actually suggested the deferral, wanting to make sure that Mia was able to play up to the school's rigorous standards, if she chose to attend.

"No," Mia had said from the center's depressing common room in that dead-flat voice she had spoken in since the accident. None of us was quite sure whether this was from emotional trauma or if this was Mia's affect now, her newly rearranged brain's way of speaking. In spite of the social worker's continued reassurances, in spite of her therapists' evaluations that she was making solid progress, we still worried. We discussed these things in hushed tones after we left her alone on the nights that I couldn't con myself into staying over.

"Well, don't be hasty," her grandmother had replied. "The world might look different in a year or two. You might still want to go."

Mia's grandmother had thought Mia was refusing Juilliard. But I knew better. I knew *Mia* better. It was the deferral she was refusing.

Her grandmother argued with Mia. September was five months away. Too soon. And she had a point. Mia's leg was still in one of those boot casts, and she was just starting to walk again. She couldn't open a jar because her right hand was so weak, and she would often blank on the names of simple things, like scissors. All of which the therapists said was to be expected and would likely pass—in good time. But five months? That wasn't long.

Mia asked for her cello that afternoon. Her grandmother had frowned, worried that this foolishness would waylay Mia's recovery. But I jumped out of my chair and ran to my car and was back with the cello by the time the sun set.

After that, the cello became her therapy: physical, emotional, mental. The doctors were amazed at Mia's upper-body strength—what her old music teacher Professor Christie had called her "cello body," broad shoulders, muscular arms—and how her playing brought that strength back, which made the weakness in her right arm go away and strengthened her injured leg. It helped with the dizziness. Mia closed her eyes as she played, and she claimed that this, along with grounding her two feet on the floor, helped her balance. Through playing, Mia revealed the lapses she tried to hide in everyday conversation. If she wanted a Coke but couldn't remember the word for it, she'd cover up and just ask for orange juice. But with cello, she would be honest about the fact that she remembered a Bach suite she'd been working on a few months ago but not a simple étude she'd learned as a child; although once Professor Christie, who came down once a week to work with her, showed it to her, she'd pick it right up. This gave the speech therapists and neurologists clues as to the hopscotch way her brain had been impacted, and they tailored their therapies accordingly.

But mostly, the cello improved her mood. It gave her

something to do every day. She stopped speaking in the monotone and started to talk like Mia again, at least when she was talking about music. Her therapists altered her rehabilitation plan, allowing her to spend more time practicing. "We don't really get how music heals the brain," one of her neurologists told me one afternoon as he listened to her play to a group of patients in the common room, "but we know that it does. Just look at Mia."

She left the rehab center after four weeks, two weeks ahead of schedule. She could walk with a cane, open a jar of peanut butter, and play the hell out of Beethoven.

⌒

That article, the "Twenty Under 20" thing from *All About Us* that Liz showed me, I do remember one thing about it. I remember the not-just-implied but overtly stated connection between Mia's "tragedy" and her "otherworldly" playing. And I remember how that pissed me off. Because there was something insulting in that. As if the only way to explain her talent was to credit some supernatural force. Like what'd they think, that her dead family was inhabiting her body and playing a celestial choir through her fingers?

But the thing was, there *was* something otherworldly that happened. And I know because I was there. I witnessed it: I saw how Mia went from being a very talented player to something altogether different. In the space of five months, something magical and grotesque transformed her. So, yes, it was all related to her "tragedy," but Mia was the one doing the heavy lifting. She always had been.

~

She left for Juilliard the day after Labor Day. I drove her to the airport. She kissed me good-bye. She told me that she loved me more than life itself. Then she stepped through security.

She never came back.

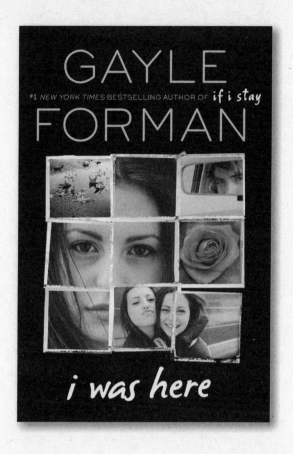

"A pitch-perfect blend of mystery, tragedy, and romance. Gayle Forman has given us an unflinchingly honest portrait of the bravery it takes to live after devastating loss."

—Stephen Chbosky, author of the #1 *New York Times* bestselling *The Perks of Being a Wallflower*

"[An] irresistible tear-jerker." —*The New York Times*

"A heartbreaking novel about coping with loss from the bestselling author of *If I Stay*." —*People*

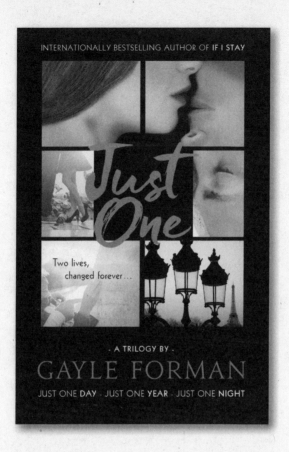

★ "Offering mystery, drama, and an evocative portrait of unrequited love, this open-ended novel will leave fans eagerly anticipating the companion story."   —*Publishers Weekly*, starred review of *Just One Day*

★ "An alluring story that pushes beyond the realm of star-crossed romance."   —*Publishers Weekly*, starred review of *Just One Year*

"Forman adds the final puzzle piece to Allyson and Willem's happily-ever-after in this euphoric e-novella . . . Fans will devour this enthralling epilogue to the duology."

—*School Library Journal* on *Just One Night*

FROM THE #1 *NEW YORK TIMES* BESTSELLING AUTHOR OF *if i stay*

**i have
lost
my way**

gayle forman

freya alone they are lost.
harun together they are found.
nathaniel ♥

"In Forman's wonderfully deft hands, this story of friendship, love, loss, and redemption becomes so much more. *I Have Lost My Way* is a beautifully written love song to every young person who has ever moved through fear and found themselves on the other side."   —Jacqueline Woodson,
author of the National Book Award winner
Brown Girl Dreaming

★ "Elegant and understated . . . A celebration of the lifesaving power of human connection."
                                          —*Publishers Weekly*, starred review